RANDOM

5-11

RANDOM

IF YOU THINK LIFE MAKES SENSE,
DO NOT READ THIS BOOK.

A NOVEL BY
Lesley Choyce

Red Deer
P R E S S

Published by
Red Deer Press
A Fitzhenry & Whiteside Company
195 Allstate Parkway,
Markham, ON L3R 4T8
www.reddeerpress.com

Edited by Peter Carver
Cover and text design by Jacquie Morris & Delta Embree, Liverpool, NS, Canada
Cover image "The Wrong Way" copyright 2008 Ryleigh Mae Anstee
Printed and bound in Canada

Acknowledgments
We acknowledge with thanks the Canada Council for the Arts, and the Ontario
Arts Council for their support of our publishing program. We acknowledge the
financial support of the Government of Canada through the Book Publishing
Industry Development Program (BPIDP) for our publishing activities.

Canada Council   Conseil des Arts
for the Arts   du Canada

ONTARIO ARTS COUNCIL
CONSEIL DES ARTS DE L'ONTARIO

Library and Archives Canada Cataloguing in Publication
Choyce, Lesley, 1951-
            Random : if you think life makes sense, do not read this book /
Lesley Choyce.
ISBN 978-0-88995-443-4
            I. Title.
PS8555.H668R35 2010   jC813'.54   C2010-904507-6

Publisher Cataloging-in-Publication Data (U.S)
Choyce, Lesley.
    Random / Lesley Choyce.
[256] p. : cm.
ISBN: 978-0-88995-443-4 (pbk.)
1. Self-perception — Juvenile fiction. I. Title.
[Fic] dc22   PZ7.C56034Ra 2010

I dedicate this book to
Jacques Snyman and Jacques Starbuck,
two fishermen who saved my daughter Sunyata
when she was swept out to sea in South Africa
in February of 2010.

CHAPTER ONE

JOSEPH HERE. JOE. SOMETIMES JOEY. THIS IS ME, TALKING INTO A digital recorder. It would shock the hell out of me if anyone ever listens to this. But it could happen. I guess anything can happen. So I will assume the remote possibility that someday I will have an audience.

But that won't change anything. I will record whatever goes through my head and talk about my life, past and present. If you want to spend your time following me, then you're along for the ride. But I promise you, this is not going anywhere. The world does not make sense. Never has, never will. I know from experience that we live through a random sequence of events and then we die.

Like my parents did—my biological parents. I was twelve at the time. My parents went to the movies. I stayed home because I had homework and I thought homework was important. The twelve-year-old me did. I was one of them. I thought things had meaning. If you worked hard, you would be rewarded. Etc. Etc.

So I stayed home. And lived. If Mr. Ogden had not assigned homework in math that day, I would not be around to share this with you. Isn't that something? Do you think Mr. Ogden knew he was saving my life when he handed us one mother of a homework assignment? He probably did this because of gas. He was always complaining of gas. Indigestion. He spoke about it often in class. He'd belch. Yes, sometimes he'd belch rather loudly. He couldn't help himself, he said. Who could ignore it? Then we'd laugh and he'd be pissed off. Then he'd get angry. And then, usually, if we laughed too hard, he'd hand down a real bitch of a homework assignment. He had a stockpile of them waiting. This is the way the sequence would go.

If there was no indigestion, no gas, no belching, then he'd assign something light for the next day. One through ten on page 125. Or no homework at all. However, on the fateful day in question, it went the other way. Gas. Belch. Laughter. Heavy-duty five-page handout—a take-home test. If you had some genius of an older brother or sister, this would not be so bad. But I was a single child.

I was a serious, responsible, single child. A single child who did not go to the movies that night so he could complete the homework. I was probably on page three of the take-home when it happened.

Later, someone pieced it together. The brake lights on my father's Ford did not work. He had said this at the dinner table. "Seal, I don't think the brake lights are working on the Ford." Seal was my mother. Celia really, but I liked it when he called her Seal. I can still picture her dark hair and black blouse and pants. She always wore black. Or white. Only black and white. Never any colors. "Seal, I don't think the brake lights are working on the Ford."

"You should get them fixed first thing tomorrow," my mom said.

And he would have.

Fixed the lights. Henry, my dad, would have fixed the goddamn lights.

But there was this movie that he was dying to see. Seal wanted to see it, too. They wanted me to come. They asked if there was any way I could finish the homework later that night or in the morning.

There wasn't. Gas is gas.

So, to cut a long story down to a short, freaking horrible truth, here goes. The garbage truck behind them did not see the brake lights when my dad hit the brakes. I learned later there had been a kid on a bicycle who had darted out into the road. He swerved away quickly, though, and rode back in the direction he had come from. Nothing happened to him. But my dad had to hit the brakes hard. Henry really pounded on those brakes. The guy driving the garbage truck—full of people's trash and heading back to the dump rather late from the day's work—was right on his ass. No lights. No extra split second to react.

A full-impact rear-ender. My dad must not have even taken his foot off the brake pedal because the car did not move forward more than a few feet.

I like the term they used in the paper: *freak accident*. Like my parents were from the circus or something. No, not that. "Freak" as in "unlikely." Spinal and neck injuries for both of a very unusual kind. Too bad that my dad had not let up on the brake. They might have rocketed forward or something and then they might have lived. I guess when Henry put on the brakes, he really meant business.

But that's the way freak accidents go. Someone standing

nearby said the boy who had been on the bike was about my age. He had been coming down from a side street—Silver Street, it was called. He didn't stop but rode that damn bike right out into the speeding traffic of Memorial Highway. But he didn't even get a nick. Then he rode away and was nowhere near the scene when the ambulance arrived.

I could tell you more about this later but it's best to just move on. I notice what I just did, by the way. I said *you*. I'm assuming, or at least pretending, that someone will hear this. I wonder why I just did that. I don't know. But then, I'm the one who does not believe that the world makes sense. There are sequences of events. Like the ones above. But there is no *meaning* to any of it. No hidden code. No purpose, I guess you could say. I will explore all of this and more, should you choose to follow me wherever this goes. And it will go into some weird shit, I promise.

So what exactly is this thing you are listening to? It's a digital recording of anything I wish to record. I chose not to write it because I don't do much writing outside of school work. Not any more. I used to like writing. I used to write essays about cures for cancer, about Leonardo da Vinci's design for helicopters, or about world over-population. I was that kind of kid. I got A's in school as well. Nothing like an A to make Henry and Seal light up. After their deaths, I gave up on most forms of communication for a while, except for screaming in my sleep. I stopped talking to people around me altogether during daylight hours. I talked to myself sometimes, however, in my bedroom at night, just to keep myself company.

And despite the fact that I didn't speak to people I knew, after sunset I phoned up random people on the phone. Yes.

Random. Straight out of the phone book. I'd pick a name, block my call and phone Jimmy Spites or Nancy Conlon. Derrick Smith-Wickens or M. Delano. These were not crank calls. This was me telling them my story.

And people listened. I never called anyone back a second time. I lied to some. I told the truth to others. A few hung up. But most did not. I like the ones who listened. I made some cry. Some were speechless. Some wondered if they should call 911 or the Help Line. No one got angry. Isn't that funny? You'd think some would be pissed off. What if I interrupted their favorite show? What if they were busy? What if they were in the middle of sex? I'm sure, given the number of calls, that at least one person answered from bed, interrupted while making love. I wondered if they could get back to it—the answerer and whomever—once they were interrupted by a twelve-year-old kid making his random call.

I sometimes told them about my parents. But not always. I made these calls for almost six months. But in the daytime, I spoke to no one. And then I got tired of it.

During that time, I remained silent to the rest of the daytime world. It was some kind of withdrawal. Some aspect of me taking control of my life. One shrink said that I should be allowed to "express myself" this way. Which is ironic—expressing yourself by not expressing yourself. Maybe I just didn't have anything to say to people I actually knew.

I stopped doing school work. I stopped laughing—at anything. Well, nothing was funny. Nothing. Not Mr. Ogden's gas. Not movies. Did I tell you my parents were driving to see a movie that my dad thought *would be really funny*? Maybe they died because they were not supposed to see a funny movie. Maybe life should be serious. Maybe that was the message. Right.

◄ ■ ►

I hope you don't mind if I jump around. Life, after all, need not be linear. Someone in a science fiction story wrote about starting your life when you die and then living it backwards from being old to being a piss-in-your pants little kid, then a vomiting baby, and then, whoopee, back into the womb. Only to start out again, dying and so forth.

My point is that without absolute meanings to things, nothing needs to be linear. Nothing *is* straightforward. Especially my narrative. I like the word "narrative." I like the way it sounds. But I don't think narrative means plot. Don't go looking for a plot here. Don't go looking for subtext or meaning. This is what it is.

Which is what? you might ask in your slightly cynical, singularly curious little mind.

My DD. My digital diary. Or a digital memoir, perhaps. I'm doing this as a birthday present to my mom. Mom-2, that is. I guess I'm doing it for Dad-2 as well, even though it isn't his birthday. They are not bad people and I will tell you about them later. They like me a lot. They adopted me after a shit load of hassles with some of my relatives. Most of my blood relatives were obnoxious, nasty people. My biological father—Bio-Dad, Dad-1, Henry—had come from what they call a very dysfunctional family, an *extended* VDF. My mom had been kicked out of her home when she was sixteen, for doing something bad she never told me about, and maybe I wouldn't have thought it was so bad at all. But after she did whatever bad thing she did, neither her parents nor anyone else in her family had wanted much to do with her. Until she died.

Then, there was insurance money and a kid. Seemed that whoever got the kid, got the cash. A kind of bad news / good news situation.

I did not want to live with any of these blood-related gobsters. Life was already hell at that point. How could it have been worse? Hell squared, I kept thinking, if any of them adopted me. Hell to the third power.

So how did I get out of that without talking to anyone? I wrote a letter. One letter to the lawyer who was overseeing my parents' estate. He then met with me and asked me about fifty yes-or-no questions to which I nodded yes or no. It was like one of those easy tests at school. You got a fifty-fifty chance of getting any question right. But apparently I aced it. Because it now meant I was up for adoption.

Think about it. I was an orphan. Like in those old stories. An orphan. But no one was going to put me in an orphanage. The lawyer turned out to be an okay guy. My bio-parents, Henry and Seal, had once said, "All lawyers are assholes," but thankfully they were wrong. Apparently, they were not right about a number of things. Brake lights needed to be fixed right away, for example, or you should not go to see light comedies on dark nights.

Henry had also thought that silver vehicles were evil. He really hated that there were so many silver cars on the road, especially SUVs. But he was wrong. Silver SUVs are not evil. Garbage trucks are evil. And kids riding bicycles on a street named Silver. Henry should have been worried about garbage trucks and kids on bikes.

My mom often talked about how she should one day patch things up with her parents, who had sent her packing. I say, no way. What parent sends away their teenage daughter? What century is this, anyway?

So there is always that right / wrong thing. Who's right and who's wrong? And who's to blame?

But it's not worth losing sleep over. The whole setup is a crap shoot. Crap, that is, like in the game. A roll of the dice. Sometimes you get seven. Sometimes, you get me. Snake eyes. Loser.

But on the next roll, I got a good lawyer and some okay parents. Which is why I am doing this for them. I am telling my story—as much as I can bear to get out of me—to a machine. DD. Hello, out there. Is anybody listening?

Dad-2 gave me the portable digital recorder with enough bytes to record twenty life stories, and I am also supposed to download the audio file onto my computer as a back-up. I'm supposed to keep back-ups in case anything goes wrong. So I do this for them. They probably think this is therapy. Which it is not. I do not want therapy. I want ... I'm not sure what I want.

I want Henry and Seal back.

But that will not happen. Not in this life. Possibly in the afterlife. If there is one. I'm not sure there is. I'm not even sure I hope there is one. If this life is so freaking difficult to understand (and for the most part, I've stopped trying), then what must the next phase be like?

◄ ■ ►

Dwelling on the past is not that wise, I've discovered. I try to live in the here and now. I'm not that big on the future, either. How can you plan a life if you know that life is a random and probably meaningless string of events? I mean, think of how illogical it all is. All the wrong people get elected, for example. You know who I'm talking about. It's kind of like high school. I mean, now that I'm sixteen, you'd think that I'd have at least partial understanding of human ways. But not me.

Take Rachelle Drummond. Beautiful, yes. But cruel. I've seen her. Voted most popular girl in school, according to last year's yearbook. I think she's actually smart but she uses her smarts for cruel things. Cheating on guys. Dumping on other girls who aren't as pretty as she is. She got caught doing something—nobody knows exactly what—with Oliver Julian in the janitor's closet. And she didn't get in trouble.

Neither did Oliver. And there's another case in point. Oliver Julian, although not handsome or smart, seems to command a lot of respect from girls, guys, and authority. He has a tidy, neat appearance, and speaks to adults with what appears to be considerable charm. But when any of them turns their back, he finds ways to humiliate people. I've been a victim more than once but I'm an easy target. He'll go after anyone, anytime, anyplace. And he enjoys it. Guess what? Voted most likely to succeed. Hah!

Look at other things. Guy invents a stupid video game, he makes millions. Guy comes up with a plan to end world hunger, he gets squat. People like Rachelle and Oliver make fun of the latter. They like to make fun of Gloria as well. Gloria Westerbend. Gloria also wants to save the world. But she's hampered by the fact that, like me, she is sixteen—although sometimes she seems much older in the way she thinks. Gloria has been trying to save me (as well as all the starving children in Africa and Asia combined) for over a year now.

Gloria is my friend. She knows my whole story. She accepts me for who I am: a non-linear, semi-atheistic, cynical, psychologically injured orphan. Well, I'm not technically an orphan anymore, thanks to Dad-2 and Mom-2. Gloria likes me despite my dark side. (Perhaps you haven't noticed my dark side yet.) And she thinks I am funny. (And I can be very funny in a non-linear, non sequitur sort of way.) Just wait till I get going. But Gloria is very, very serious.

I don't know why people get so serious. It seems like a lot of work and worry and, ultimately, disappointment. It's like the Glorias of the world are hoping to spruce things up, solve a few global issues, give hope and help and ultimately get ignored (if they're lucky) or labeled as fringe radicals and arrested if they are not. While the Olivers and Rachelles of the world go on to win large sums of money and fame on so-called reality-based TV shows and then start their own designer labels for hideous clothing with their names on them.

For a while I had this grand plan to collect dog shit and find ways to put it in locations where both Oliver and Rachelle would step in it. I confess I had some fun (rare, but there it is) thinking about this. Just suppose the two of them kept stepping into dog crap over and over again. Wouldn't that be interesting? I mean, really.

But I could never bring myself to execute the plan. Reason being I do not have a dog and I do not want to collect the necessary elements to execute the plan. So the two of them go through life without having the hassle of scraping it out of the tread of their fashionable shoes. Maybe when I'm older,

I'll come up with an adult version of this to execute, once the golden boy and girl have attained star status.

So have you had enough of me already? Odd but interesting? Or just demented? Most everyone has written me off in one way or another. All except for my current parents. And Gloria. And, of course, Dean.

CHAPTER TWO

I GUESS I SHOULD TELL YOU ABOUT MY CURRENT PARENTS. MY FATHER'S name is Willard but he is known as Will. Mom is Beth. Will and Beth MacDonald. They were incredibly brave in adopting me. Can you imagine? *We have this twelve-year-old kid who is probably scarred for life and if he turns out the slightest bit normal, we will all be shocked.* I think the social worker said something like that.

"We want the kid," my father would have said. "We want to help."

"We can handle this," my mom would have added. "We can make this work." Or so I envision the conversation.

I'm sure my many months of silence freaked them out, but I'm also certain my dad put a good spin on it. "He never complains," my dad would have told his colleagues. "And he has good eating habits."

The eating habit part would have been important to Will. After all, he owns a health food store. He's big on vegetables and positively anything organic. And I was willing to eat whatever he set in front of me. Kale, for example. My dad was thrilled that I would eat kale. And if I ever seemed unhappy or unhealthy, he would say something like, "I don't think Joseph is getting enough selenium." Or he'd try to feed me wild salmon from Alaska. "Omega-3 always does the trick." I never complained about the fish, either.

Maybe that's why I never get sick. My selenium levels are way up there. The kale wards off diphtheria and cholera and those diseases spread by chickens from China. And the salmon helps, too. "A good diet can allow you to live to be a hundred. Easily," Dad would say.

I'm not sure I want to live to be a hundred, though. A hundred is eighty-four years away. I'm more of a one-day-at-a-time kind of person. There are so many pluses and minuses in life, if you know what I mean. Sometimes there seem to be more minuses and, on those days, despite my good diet and great health, I don't feel like getting out of bed. I'm sure you know what that feels like.

So my dad hopes that one day I'll take over the health food store. It's called Nature's Bounty. I can't envision myself running Nature's Bounty. I work there part-time, though, and it's kind of weird. Women ask me which of the vitamins will help them lose weight. I don't know if vitamins help you lose weight but I pick up a plastic container of expensive vitamins with a picture of a thin woman on it. "Take one a day," I say. "Drink a lot of water and eat fresh vegetables. Kale is good for losing weight. It has a lot of selenium in it and it's excellent roughage." My dad talks a lot about roughage so I'm sort of borrowing from him.

Men come into the store sometimes and wander around looking for something. They look nervous and uncomfortable. At first I thought they were trying to steal something but I soon began to understand what they were looking for. "I'm looking for something to restore ... my vitality," they might say and I'd give the same routine about vitamins, kale, water, and maybe show them some Omega-3 and a men's vitamin with a healthy-looking older dude on it.

"Well," one of them might say, "not just my vitality but my youth."

"Hmm."

"My libido."

"Duh?"

Then the whisper. "I'm talking about sex."

"Oh."

I didn't know about all the stuff in the store. I didn't know there were health store pills for sex. All I'd ever heard about was Viagra and we didn't sell that.

"Have you tried ginseng?" I asked.

"No. Is it good?"

"Good. Are you kidding? It's great." I made it sound like I was taking ginseng and getting laid all the time.

"I'll take some."

I asked my dad later about this and he told me there were supplements in the store that I could steer customers to next time. "Ginseng might help," he said. "At least it can't hurt. But next time you can steer them toward the horny goat weed."

I laughed. "No way!"

"Way," he said. "That's what it's called. They say it really works—on goats, at least." He smiled.

So the next time I saw a male customer lurking around, I steered him straight down the aisle to the horny goat weed. I even steered some of the men looking to lose weight to the horny goat weed. "Nothing helps you to lose weight better," I'd say to them, "than a lot of sex."

Not that I know that much about sex. I'm more or less on the sidelines in that department. Sex is for people like Oliver and Rachelle. I've tried talking about sex with Gloria, the oh-so serious one, but she is, alas, so serious. And I'm kind of shy in that department. Sometimes I wonder what would happen if I took some horny goat weed. But I'm too scared to try. I've read in a magazine about the possible side effects of Viagra, for example. Some men end up in the hospital. They get up but they can't get back down. And that would be kind of embarrassing, if you get my drift.

But enough about sex.

My mother is an investment counselor with the bank. She thinks selenium is something you should invest in, I think. And platinum. And gold. She's not that thrilled with silver right now. "Silver is in a slump," I heard her say to one of her clients on the phone. "But molybdenum is hot." Molybdenum is a metal used in a lot of high-tech stuff, in case you haven't heard. It could be what they call "the next big thing." But Beth, like my dad, is also environmentally conscious, so she only recommends investing in companies that are environmentally friendly. Since many mining companies are notorious for raping and pillaging the earth, I would think this is a damn hard thing to do.

She sometimes uses investment terminology when referring to our family but, don't get me wrong, she's a great mother. "We took a bit of a gamble on you," she once said about me. "We knew there would be some short-term volatility but the long term looked good. I think we made a wise move."

They couldn't have children of their own. Some problem

with my mother's eggs. There was no health store cure for it and they'd tried fertility clinics. They were thinking about adopting a girl from China when I came along.

I've always felt a little guilty about that. There is some orphan girl in China who did not get adopted because of me. If I had been in the car with my bio-parents, this small bit of history would have turned out much differently.

My mother took off from work for three months when I was adopted. So did my dad. Will and Beth were worried and tried everything to make me feel at home. It took a while but I got on with my life. I try not to revisit those deep, dark places where I could go if I let myself. Somewhere down the line, I may explore the past to learn more about my bio-parents, Henry and Seal, but not yet. It may turn ugly for me and I don't want ugly in my life right now. And it could be that I may never go there to explore the pain of losing my parents. I don't know what the future will bring. And I don't want to know.

None of us knows about the future. I can live with that. I'm not one of those kids with hopes and aspirations. I don't want to be famous or rich. I don't want to invent things or do good deeds. I'd like to have sex with a girl before I leave high school, but I don't have much of a plan in that regard. I just don't want to be like one of those men lurking around the health food store, waiting to discover horny goat weed in order to have a sex life.

Now I know I should be calling it "making love" and not just "having sex." I haven't sorted out the love / sex thing yet. Some things take time.

◄ ■ ►

The purpose of the digital diary, as I understand it, is to understand who I am. That is, who I am now; who I am now is quite different from who I was five years ago. Who I am today is not even the same as who I was yesterday. Everything keeps changing. The world is in "flux." The world, as I see it, is fluxed.

And it is in need of a good revolution. A turning. A change. A big transformation that no one sees coming. There is a theory called the "foco theory." (You may soon discover that I am a big fan of theories and ideas and unusual terms. Both of my bio-parents liked to use the word theory, beginning sentences like this: "In theory, that would be the right thing to do, but in reality ..." Even when I was young, one or the other was referring to some theory they had read about. Once they were both gone, I found myself looking up all kinds of theories to try to help explain what the hell was going on in the world. There was never any philosophical or scientific theory that made perfect sense, but each new theory I glommed onto added something to my understanding—or lack thereof—of the forces at work around me.) But I digress.

According to foco theory, a small group of very animated people can make society change in a radical way. You do not have to wait for conditions to create a demand for change. This small but hardy group of excitable humans can inspire and ignite an uprising, and change will occur.

They say this is what happened in Cuba. Che Guevara (1928–1967) and his followers did just that. Foco revolution. The Americans did not like this little bit of history. World in flux. I don't know what happened to Che Guevara but I think he died. And Cuba changed. But Cuba did not change the world.

Of course, you might also have to take into account the so-called "least effort principle," put forward by an American shrink with the very cool name of G.K. Zipf. He came to the conclusion that animals, and probably all organisms when confronted with several choices, tend to pick the one that requires the least effort. He studied rats to come up with this rather obvious theory. So, if your teacher says you have the option of doing your homework or not doing your homework, and either way you get an A, which would you choose? The one that requires the least effort, of course.

Revolutions, as Che Guevara and others discovered, take a lot of effort. So you have to work damn hard, I'd say, to get people worked up enough to join your revolution. I myself have not selected what kind of revolution I'd put forward. Not yet, anyway. But I am thinking about it. The only problem is that I have very few social skills and even fewer friends. Gloria would, of course, help me with my revolution if it were a good cause. But I don't think I am that type. I think my first revolution would just be designed to remove Monday from the days of the week. Mondays bite.

◄ ■ ►

My parents worry that I might not be able to find my way in the world. They recognize my confusion. My lack of focus. My non-linear way of living my life. I do not select my clothes in the morning, for example. My clothes select me. I close my eyes and reach into my closet and whichever shirt wants to be worn, it directs my hand to it. Same for pants. I call it automatic dressing. Some of the combinations are odd but I never second-guess my clothing. Even socks. If two socks don't match, I wear them anyway. This used to produce results quite amusing to my classmates, but now my mom sneaks into my room and pairs my socks, like a medieval matchmaker.

At school, I make a point of saying hello to random people at random times. I sometimes ignore kids I actually know and instead say, "Hey, how's it going?" to guys and girls I have never spoken to before. The results are interesting. One older guy from twelfth grade called me a "homo." In his mind, an unknown male student saying hello indicates homosexuality. Seems perfectly logical to me.

A science teacher, Ms. Mallory, seemed impressed by my random hello. When she saw me again, she said hello to me and asked me my name. Joseph, I told her. Joseph Campbell. "*The* Joseph Campbell?" she said. I didn't know what she meant by that but I said, "Yes, *the* Joseph Campbell," and decided to take her biology class the next year because she showed an interest in me and because she had nice legs. Am I a total perv because I like science teachers with great legs?

I gave Oliver my random hello once. He and I are not exactly breathing any of the same oxygen or even abiding on nearby planets. He just snarled. I forgot about snarling. It was pretty fascinating. He snarled just like Mr. Langford's Rottweiler down the street. What should a person who is tossing around a thousand theories in his head make of that?

And the girls who get the random hi—the "howzitgoing-today?"—mostly don't seem to mind. I look them in the eye for effect and they smile. Some flutter their eyelashes, which I find way cool. Some say, "Oh, hi," in a polite, shy fashion.

They don't actually stop and have a conversation with me or anything. Only one girl got mad. Rachelle's friend, Destiny. Her response was, "What drugs are you on?"

So, as you can see, this all goes into my digital diary. I am doing this for my parents because they took a big chance adopting me. But my DD is not—I repeat, not—for my parents to listen to. It is for you, some random you, whoever you are, who I may or may not know. My perfect audience of one. Or none, as the case may be.

But, like I said, my parents asked me to do this because they thought it would be good for me. So I am doing it. I owe them big time. As you can imagine, they want me to be happy. They want me to be normal. I'm happy sometimes but that, too, seems to happen at random times.

I even have golden moments. I didn't know what those golden moments were until I was reading a rather randomly picked book from the library about eastern religions. I discovered the word that Japanese Zen Buddhists have for those splashes of euphoria. The word is *satori*. And here's the kicker. For me, they seem to happen for no apparent reason whatsoever. Surprise, surprise.

I'll be sitting through history class on a day dull as dirty dishwater and suddenly I'll feel cheerful. I'll feel okay. I'll feel happy to be alive. And I don't know why. Or I'll be walking down Gordon Street with a tune in my head, something by the False Prophets, when it kicks in. Once it even happened when I was thinking about my childhood. I had this perfect memory of being maybe five years old, sitting on the grass, playing with some round stones I was collecting. My bio-parents were there, kind of out of focus in the bright sun, but there nonetheless. And it was all so real. And then it was gone. And I cried.

The hard part of any *satori* is coming back down. I didn't tell my current parents about the memory because, when I do stuff like that, my mom cries and then my dad cries. My dad never cries first. Usually it's mom and then dad. First her and then him.

CHAPTER THREE

MY PARENTS DON'T WORRY AS MUCH ABOUT ME AS THEY DID WHEN I was younger. I don't know what they thought I would do. But they worried a lot, for sure. Beth gave me books to read that had hopeful messages. *Chicken Soup for the Teenage Soul. Cream of Mushroom Soup for the Angst-Ridden Adolescent, Broth for the Brainless*, and other ones. *Maximize your Happiness*, I think, was the name of one. A couple of financial titles like *Think and Grow Rich* or *Mind over Money*. My mom isn't all that greedy but she has a thing about money. She likes the way it moves. It makes sense to her and she is a sober and steady investment counselor.

My mom helps people who save money and invest it wisely. She even invested $5,000 in a trust fund for me when I was adopted and it is now worth $25,000.

"How come it's worth so much?" I asked one morning at breakfast.

"Because we did nothing," she answered, and then promptly rushed off to work—presumably to counsel other young parents about making money by doing nothing. "That's the trick," I could hear her say. "The trick is doing nothing."

I told her, "Mom, you should write a book called *The Art of Doing Nothing* or *The Science of Doing Nothing Well.*" I understand this could have a double meaning, though. After she had breezed out of the kitchen and off to her enclave of negative optimal capitalism (I just made that up) my dad, peering up at me through his Harry-Potter-round wire-rimmed glasses, tried to explain to me what she does at work.

"Your mom is like a gardener," he explained. "It's like she plants the seeds and then lets the rain and sunshine do all the work. But you need good seeds, good soil, lots of sun, and patience." So the seeds were the money, the soil was the economy, the sun was, I guess, good economic growth, and patience was, well, patience. I needed to translate for myself since my dad was mostly an organic farmer at heart even though he didn't have an organic farm. "She got excited about platinum a long time ago," he added. "And zinc. I never knew someone could get so excited about zinc. But she always bought and just held on." He grasped some imaginary thing in front of him so that he was holding out two fists. But it wasn't nasty fists. It was just grasping imaginary bars of platinum and zinc.

"Don't you sell zinc in the health food store?"

"Yes. It wards off colds and other diseases."

"Is it as good as selenium?"

"Both are good for you in the proper doses. Too much of either and you could be in trouble, though."

"Too much of anything and you could be in trouble," I added, trying to keep up my end of the conversation.

I must have looked sad, though, because next my dad raised his glasses up onto his forehead and asked, "Is everything okay at school?"

"School is school," I answered. I could have added, "Life is life," or "It is what it is," or any number of inane things I was prone to saying.

"I hear you," he said. "I know what you're saying," intoned as if he was one of my friends—of which there were very few. Well, two, really.

My father sat there looking at me until he realized I felt uncomfortable, so he went back to dipping into a bowl of muesli and organic Balkan yogurt. He had told me once that yogurt, Balkan yogurt with real live bacterial culture, was what allowed some people in the Balkans to remain healthy and strong well into old age.

I dipped into my own bowl of muesli. *Thirty-five percent nuts and fruits,* it said on the box—"just like school," I once said to my dad when I was helping to restock the shelves of the store and I was trying to be funny—which was not all that often. I wondered again what it would be like to live to a hundred. Living till that old was not high on my list of wishes. Living to sixteen seemed rough enough. Not that I wanted to off myself. Nothing like that. It just seemed that living to be a hundred could become a bit of a chore. What would you do with all those hours and days and years?

Do nothing, my mother might say—which, of course, did not mean to be lazy or negative or unambitious. Financially, if I leave that $25,000 "doing nothing," it will be worth several million dollars by the time I am a hundred. But then what? What does a centenarian do with a fortune? Go looking for the aisle with the ginseng and horny goat weed?

I dutifully shoveled another spoonful of yogurt and muesli down and pondered all this. Pondering often made me look unhappy, I think.

"Are you okay?" my dad asked, for maybe the millionth time in my life.

I was thinking about another bit of advice I'd come across, on a random Web site that I had stumbled onto with a Google search. Whoever had posted the site, a guy known to his Internet audience simply as Ron advocated music, sex, and beer as the three key elements to happiness and longevity. Ron had a picture of himself on the site. He looked to be about fifty. He was bald but had hair coming up from around the collar of his shirt, so he must have had one hell of a lot of chest hair. And he did look happy. Maybe he would write a book some day. *Chicken Soup for the Horny, Drunken Music Lover's Soul.*

To answer my father's much repeated question, I said, "Does anyone actually know when they are okay?"

He studied me again. "Yeah, sometimes they do. You will, too. I promise."

As you might have noticed, I have a fascination with words. I notice that most kids at school use the same words and phrases over and over. People tend to be very lazy when it comes to vocabulary, but when I hear a new word, I want to know its meaning. We had a substitute teacher, a young guy just out of university called Philip Bird. He wanted us to call him Phil. He took over teaching history from Mr. Briar. Briar had one of those mid-career breakdowns that comes from teaching history for twenty years to teenagers who have no interest in anything that occurred in the world, no matter how momentous, before the previous week. We all saw it coming, but those who had been unkind to Briar remained so up until the end, up until he cracked. Poor Mr.

Briar cracked like an egg, right there in class. "You idiots don't give a rat's ass about the Versailles Treaty, do you?" This is what a history teacher says when he is losing it. His shell. His marbles. His cool. His twenty-year record of never going nuts during school hours.

I had tried giving a rat's ass about the Versailles Treaty but there were a lot of hands in that pie and I couldn't keep all the players straight. Everybody wanted something and they went about dividing up Europe (including the yogurt-eating Balkaners) and the Middle East and Africa. In the right frame of mind, it could have been quite fascinating. But no, we didn't have a rodent's derriere of interest in any treaties on Mr. Briar's thorny curriculum.

I don't blame him for going nuts. He had his say and then left the room, slamming the door. And everyone in the class (except me, of course, and Gloria) looked at each other like, *What did we do? It wasn't our fault.* Gloria and I understood Briar's plight and his exodus. And we both felt kind of bad about it. Gloria, for her part, was getting an A in the course and wrote great papers about political shifts in Europe. My papers rambled, as you can imagine, but I did at least "show some effort," as Briar noted in the margins.

The way I showed effort was by bullshitting. I can't find any other word that describes what I did. I did not usually read the textbook or pay close attention to the lectures but, instead, I'd write convoluted, cryptic answers that would achieve a C, which gives you an idea as to how bad the other papers must have been, papers and the student thinking be-hind them so bad that it would drive any high school history teacher to succumb to madness.

The instruction might read like this: *Explain how the Treaty of Versailles set in motion the major political changes across Europe in the decades after it was signed.* My answer would begin something like this:

> *There is no doubt that the Treaty of Versailles, one of the most significant and profound treaties of the twentieth century, set in motion a chain of events that could not have been foreseen by the architects of this document. The treaty purported to solve one set of political and economic problems, but while failing to do that, it created other more numerous crises that swept the continent and led to unrest, dissent, squabbling, and ultimately war. Critics of the treaty say it unleashed havoc on the modern world in an unprecedented way that could have been avoided, had more forethought and less self-serving ambitions come into play.*

I need not torture you further, but as you can see, I was skillful with words while being somewhat short on any actual concrete information. That's what a bullshitter does on a test. He bullshits. And like I said, I like words, so I could nail down a C on most any subject and garner that slightly complimentary comment of at least "showing some effort."

But just as the Treaty of Versailles was certain to fail and lead Europe into another world war, so, too, was Briar certain to reach his breaking point. Gloria wrote him a get well card that read, "Hope you get well soon," and I signed it at her request.

I am reporting all this here in my digital diary to illustrate to anyone who listens to this what kind of student I was and provide some insight into the education of my day.

Anyhow, Phil Bird flew into the classroom the first day of his substitute stint with great enthusiasm coupled with the kind of polished naïveté and idealism that can only come from lack of actual teaching experience.

He had longish hair, a mustache, and a goatee like I'd seen in old paintings. He read out our names and looked each of us in the eye. I liked the fact that he used big words.

"Twentieth-century history," he announced, reminding us all of what class this was. "A century is a hundred years. A lot can happen in a hundred years." Some rolled their eyes at such an obvious observation. "In French, century is called *siècle*, in Italian it is *secolo*, in Czech it is *století*, and in German *Jahrhundert*." This didn't seem to have much to do with anything, but maybe he just wanted to show off his knowledge of European languages. Next he proceeded to give us the tallies of the dead in at least a dozen European countries, resulting from the First World War. He had them memorized. "The War to End All Wars, they called it," he said. "In many parts of Europe, it set in motion a kind of nihilism that would have devastating results." I had said as much in my paper, I realized. But I had not used that word. And a very good word it was. *Nihilism*. Bird pronounced it "Nigh-hill-izm."

Before I could muster the energy or courage to ask what the word meant, Gloria had already put her hand up. "What does nihilism mean?" she asked.

Bird fluttered a bit and seemed to puff up with an exaggerated intake of the school's oxygen supply. "It's a kind of negative philosophy. You could say it is a denial of beliefs, traditions, and meaning. It is a rejection of order and, well, everything—a rejection of what others believe. It suggests that nothing in our lives has any meaning or value. Some would call it a belief in nothing."

Clearly, this was a different sort of nothing from my mother's investment code where doing nothing amounted to something like, in her world, creating wealth. In the European world, belief in nothing, rejection of everything, led to bloodshed and horrors. But that was then. This was now. Having heard the word for the first time, I realized that I was a kind of nihilist myself. I wasn't the vengeful, hating kind. I was just the teenage, confused, nerdy kid kind. I had emptied myself of many of the tried and true kid things to believe in and was now living my small open-ended and confused life. I was not using my nihilism to do anything bad ... or good, for that matter. I was just waiting for something to happen.

And I had no idea what that something was.

CHAPTER FOUR

In the nineteenth century, scientists believed in the conservation of matter principle. Matter could not be created or destroyed. But it could change. They also believed that energy could not be created or destroyed. It just changed form as well. Then Einstein came along with the theory that matter could change to energy and energy to matter, and he formulated the famous $E=mc^2$ thing. Still seems that nothing goes away; it just changes form. I'm not sure why I care about any of this but I do.

For so long I had tried to make sense of the world and it didn't seem to be going anywhere. Living was all about loss. $L=lss^2$. I invested four years of my life into that formula along with the one $MOL=0$ (meaning of life equals zero). The best-selling title would be *Cold Chicken Shit Soup for the Teenage Loser*.

This all could get dark and depressing if it weren't for the fact that Gloria came into my life. Gloria is my closest friend. I can't call her my girlfriend, exactly. I don't kiss her or take her on dates. I like Gloria for her mind. And her loyalty. She is loyal to me, no matter how moody I am. Gloria as in "glory."

The *Oxford English Dictionary* has nearly half a column with definitions for "glory," but I most like the one that says, "resplendent beauty and magnificence." Resplendent is a very good word and so is magnificence. I think there is a term in the Bible (not that I spend much time reading it) that uses the phrase "Gloria in Excelsis," as in glory in the highest ... or most excellent.

Gloria keeps her beauty hidden. She's one of those girls. She keeps her hair tied up. She wears glasses with plastic rims. She does not wear makeup. She doesn't seem to care what clothes she chooses in the morning to wear. (Maybe she, too, is an automatic dresser.) She walks funny and sits kind of slouched over. She is probably the smartest girl in the school. *Gloria in Excelsis.*

Gloria seeks me out in the hallways and sits with me in the cafeteria. Sometimes she doesn't say much or speak at all. She loans me money to buy junk food. Or at least she did until they removed all the junk food from the cafeteria. Now you can't even buy potato chips or candy at school. What's this world coming to, anyway?

The first day I discovered there were no more chips, I was pissed.

Gloria actually held my hand in hers and looked into my eyes. "This is all an illusion, anyway," she told me. "This is just the surface of things. The real world is something else."

"What something else?"

"I don't know for sure. But it's there inside your heart," she said. This is the way she speaks.

"Then there's still junk food in the real world?"

"Probably," she said. "All things are possible."

Now, a statement like "All things are possible" is probably directly in opposition to my entrenched nihilism. The motto of my club was: nothing is possible. Don't believe in anything. Gloria, while having no single religious or philosophical inclination, had a very open view of what was possible. I could call her a naïve optimist. Actually that *is* what I called her.

"You're just a naïve optimist," I said, even though she was still holding my hand and I liked holding hers. She did not pull her hand away. She looked deeper into my eyes. "Thank you," she said. "I'll take that as a compliment." Then she let go of me and reached into her backpack, retrieving a candy bar. She handed it to me. An Oh Henry. The name on the wrapper made a wave of dizziness go through me. I closed my eyes for a second. Saw my father. Dad-1. He was a bit of a candy freak. I guess I had never told Gloria about that.

"Are you okay?" Gloria asked.

"Sure," I said. I didn't want to get into it. I unwrapped the candy and ate it.

"Watch out for the sugar rush," she said. Gloria was eating a tofu and spinach sandwich that she had made herself. It must have been her mom who had put the Oh Henry bar in her bag. Gloria and my current father would have a lot in common.

◄ ■ ►

Gloria gets depressed a lot. Like I said, she takes everything too seriously. Unlike me. When life gives you a lemon, I say, step on it and make it squirt. When it gives you chicken bones, make chicken soup. When it gives you ... well, you get the picture. This does not make me an optimist, though. Please. Cheerful optimists, the type I find at school, can be so annoying. It's like they think everything is for the good. Like there is some grand plan. Some meaning. Some purpose.

Not me. I won't be fooled by such tricks of the brain. Life is meaningless and I move on from there. But I don't get depressed about that fact if I can help it. The trick is not to care too deeply about anything and not to take anything too seriously. Then you don't crack like Mr. Briar or blather on like Phil Bird. And you don't get depressed like Gloria Westerbend.

But what if I told you I'd be lost without Gloria? Would that surprise you? This must mean I care about her. And I do. How can a nihilist care about anything? you might ask. Call it a paradox, if you like. The world still makes no sense but I care about Gloria. So when she gets depressed, I get worried.

Right after the Oh Henry bar, she suddenly got quiet. Quiet like the way Dean gets quiet. (More on Dean later.) Gloria sat staring at the wall as I chewed the candy bar. I didn't have to ask.

"It's my parents," she said. "They love each other."

"That's a good thing, right?" I asked.

"Yes and no. They love each other but they fight all the time. They disagree on everything."

"But they love each other?"

"Yes."

"That's the way it goes sometimes," I said, way too casually. To me, such illogic made perfect sense—in a world where nothing made sense, if you get my drift.

"But these are my parents."

"And you'd like to see them happy."

"Yes."

"But now their unhappiness has made you unhappy. And that's not good. Gloria, you are too sensitive. You can't make them happy. You can't stop them from arguing."

"Do your parents argue?"

"Sometimes they argue over which brand of laundry detergent is least harmful to the environment."

"That's not an argument," she said.

"Then what constitutes an argument?"

"My mom says she wished she'd never met my father. She says it ruined her life."

"That's a large generalization. Probably unfair."

"Then my father says he should have gone to Spain. He always wanted to move to Spain."

"Why Spain?"

"Barcelona. He wanted to live in Barcelona."

"And if he had moved to Barcelona, I would not be having this conversation with you, would I?"

"No. Everything would have been different."

"And you would not have existed," I said. And now I felt sad. Wow. I'd be sitting here alone, probably, no Oh Henry bar, no junk food. No Gloria. "Listen, all we can do is live in the present," I said, probably quoting from one of those books my mom gave me. I guess for all my weirdness, I did believe in that. Living in the present. The good and the bad. Not trying to feel too bad about the past or too anxious about the future. The good old here and now.

Gloria was staring at the wall. I'd seen her do this too many times before. She was going away somewhere. And this was not good. I couldn't come up with the code to break the silence. And it's funny how silent and empty everything seemed, because the cafeteria was filled with noise.

"What about your first parents?" she asked.

"Henry and Seal?" I hadn't said their names out loud in a long time. "What about them?"

"Did they ever argue?"

I thought about it. I don't think I had any memories left of them arguing. They must have, but I erased them. Or maybe they never did argue. Maybe they loved each other so much that they were incapable of arguing. "Yes," I said, however, hoping it would help Gloria. "They had arguments like umpires and baseball coaches. They used bad language. The neighbors were appalled."

"But they loved each other?"

"Of course." Now I was the one feeling sad. Anything that conjured up my bio-parents took me toward a dark, cold room inside me. Gloria's depression was now contagious.

"I'm sorry," she said. "I shouldn't have asked that." She looked away to the wall again for a second, but then looked back at me. Soft, sad eyes. She took off her glasses and I was reminded how pretty she really was.

"Thanks for the Oh Henry," I said. I wanted to take Gloria's hand and lead her outside into the sunlight. I wanted to run with her down the street, like we were little kids running away. Running away from the world. I wanted to save her, I guess.

But I didn't do that. I wasn't that kind of person.

◀ ■ ▶

I don't know who invented the idea of school. Plato? Socrates? I don't know who to blame.

My point being that school does not work. A teacher in a room with twenty to thirty students with attention spans of about thirty-five seconds. Three minutes tops. After that, it's all daydreaming about anything but school. The bell rings and you move on to another subject where you get your good thirty-five seconds of learning before you start to drift.

I'm a drifter. I settle into my seat, become lulled by the weary tones of my instructor, and then move on to some other realm. I prefer beaches and oceans. So I go there. Or mountains and forests. I go there, too. Or girls. Sometimes there are girls there. Imaginary ones that I have never met.

I am drifting to islands with palm trees and white sandy beaches when Dean passes me a note.

Dude, do you think we'll be able to visit Mars in our lifetime?

That's what Dean is thinking about. Travel to other planets. I write back on the piece of paper. *The moon, maybe. Probably not Mars.* I slip it over to his desk while the teacher has her back turned. Dean looks disappointed.

I have not told you anything about Dean. Dean is on his own planet, as you can imagine. I wonder if Dean will have a chance to visit Earth in his lifetime. Dean perhaps was given a tad too much Ritalin when he was growing up. I remember him as a wiry, weird, and wired young kid who liked to ride his bicycle straight into the lake on purpose and shoot peas out of his nose during meals. He drank a lot of Kool-Aid and gave teachers a really hard time in school. And then he was medicated.

He stopped shooting peas out of his nose, no more bike trips into cold water, and his teachers reported he was "more polite" in school. Before Dean settled down, and back before I lost my first set of parents, we roamed the woods, skate-boarded in the parking lots, and rode our bikes to the lake (and he *into* the lake). And then I went through my thing. And Dean. Dean settled down. And, like me, was never quite the same again. So we share that. We were both someone else at one point.

Dude, the next note said, *what about the Russians? You can pay to go up in space, right? Have you ever checked into the fares?*

He used the word *fare* like it would have been posted on Expedia or something. One way to the space station so much. Return fare, so much. Did they have first class and economy or just one price? Did you get a free meal or just a bag of nuts?

I smiled and wrote back. *Dude, it's gotta be very expensive. Start saving your quarters.* I slipped it to him.

He smiled. He was satisfied with my answer.

CHAPTER FIVE

DID YOU EVER THINK ABOUT THE WORD "DILEMMA?" I DISCOVERED THAT the true meaning of the word is a problem with two unpleasant solutions. This means you get in a screwed-up situation and you have two choices for finding a way out. Neither one is good but you do have to choose one. Whichever one you pick, somebody or something pays. They use the phrase that you are on "the horns of a dilemma." Makes it sound like an animal—a bull or a moose, maybe.

I think a lot of life is like that. You have to choose. You have no choice. But it's not always easy and you pay. Back then, after the accident, the doctor on my case wanted to put me on some kind of medication. "It will ease the pain," he said. "It will get you through it." I don't know why I chose not to do this. I think I was just stubborn. And the truth is this: I wanted to feel the pain. And feel it I did.

The new parents coming on board helped get my head back into the so-called real world. I had drifted off to very, very distant islands and forests and mountains. Big time. Will and Beth MacDonald walked the wilderness until they found me and brought me back. I still don't know how they did that. But the pain was still with me. Will always be with me.

So what do you do to get through your life, making sure

that you never have to feel that sort of pain again? Well, you try not to care so bloody much about anything.

And I've tried that. In fact, I'm still doing it. But that's one of those dilemma situations, too. You protect yourself, but you sacrifice as well.

Dean calls me up and wants to know if I think he should be a marine biologist. "Someone has to look out for the fish," he says.

"Dude, I think you'd make a great marine biologist. You'd get a boat. Hire some really cute girls—cute but really smart and eco-friendly—to work with you and you go do your thing."

"I'd really like to study the Mariana Trench."

I knew that the Mariana Trench was possibly the deepest part of any ocean on earth.

"It'll be pretty dark down there."

"I'm okay with dark."

"And such a long way down."

"A lot of pressure, I know."

"But if that is what you want to study, you should go for it."

"Maybe I will. I was just watching a documentary on the Discovery Channel and it kind of made me think this is my life's calling."

"How are you doing in biology?"

"Not all that great."

"Then you might need to try harder. What about math?"

"I think I'm passing."

"Passing is good."

"Thanks, dude. I just needed to call and run this past you."

"No problem."

"Did you know that Mars has two moons?"

"No," I said. "I didn't know that."

"Phobos and Deimos."

"How'd you know that?"

"Everybody knows that."

"Right."

That was a fairly typical Dean phone call. I don't know what will become of the Deans of the world. I think they need to be protected—like an endangered species. Dean is vulnerable, as you can imagine. The Oliver Julians of the world love to make fun of him. He's easy to make fun of. It's not that he's stupid. In fact, I think he's quite smart. He just fell off the truck and the truck moved on—figuratively speaking. I hope he wins the lottery, gets rich, and blows it all on a trip with the Russians to the space station where he falls in love with a very beautiful and loving lady Russian cosmonaut (if they're still called cosmonauts), who is there observing the two moons of Mars. I hope they get married on a boat floating above the Mariana Trench back on earth and have some really cool, happy kids. That's what I hope.

◄ ■ ►

Dreams and aspirations. An interesting combination of words. It's also a title of the False Prophets first album. The concept is all about what if. What if we got to live out our dream? What if we got to do what we really want to do in life? Would there still have to be dilemmas? Probably.

It was my mom today who initiated the career conversation with me. It must be Career Week in the world. "Any ideas what you want to do with your life, Joe?" It was breakfast. I'm not that awake at breakfast. Neither was my dad. My dad just looked down at his muesli.

"Dean says he wants to be a marine biologist," I said. "Maybe I'll do that. He and I can be a team."

"How is Dean?" Will asked, trying to change the subject.

"Dean is Dean."

Dad-2 nodded. Mom-2 paused and then proceeded. "You can take over the store if that seems to be your calling."

Will nodded again, smiled. I knew that had always been his dream, but he knew it might not be mine. "I like the store," I said. "Maybe that will work out."

"We're moving into more fresh fruits and vegetables," my dad said, still smiling. Fewer jars with vitamins and pills. More fresh mesclun (which are greens, by the way, not drugs) and pomegranates. I tried to contain my excitement.

"Well, I'm just trying to get through high school," I said.

"Understood," my mom said.

Will and Beth both looked caringly at their adopted son and you could tell they were worried about him.

So, during school that day, I, too, began to puzzle over me. What if I did not "find my place in the world?" Certainly I would not be alone. Dean would probably be there with me. And Gloria, maybe. Gloria, like Dean, was fragile. Would she ever be able to survive out there? School is bad enough. But everything after that could be so difficult. And what about me? Would the world let me drift? Let me daydream? I truly had no ambition to be a marine biologist. Someone else would have to save the jellyfish and the shrimp. I couldn't see myself as a teacher or an investment counselor. And I guess the store was a fallback position. But a life among vegetables and fruits? I don't know.

◄ ■ ►

Alternate time line. "If you see a fork in the road, take it." According to baseball legend, Yogi Berra said that. I'm not sure I know who Yogi Berra is but it's funny. Daydreaming today in health class, right when I should have been paying attention to information about the endocrine system— which may be of use to me someday—I came to the fanciful conclusion that there is another time line with another me somewhere. I don't know where, just somewhere, even if it is just in my head.

The other me is, of course, the one who did not lose his first set of parents to a garbage truck. Henry and Seal came home that night and they had a small argument. Yes, they were arguing about the movie. But I can't remember the name of the movie. I had finished my homework for Mr. Ogden and was watching a rerun of a TV sitcom. I was tired and almost asleep. I asked my parents about the film. "How was it?"

"I didn't like the ending," my mother said. "It was unrealistic."

"How else could they end it?" my father said, sounding a little miffed. This was quite unusual for them.

"Let's just go to bed," my mom said. And they went to bed.

I turned off the TV, brushed my teeth, and went to bed. As if nothing had happened.

Because nothing *had* happened. No crash, no ambulance, no cop at the door near midnight. In the morning, whatever little disagreement had existed between my parents had ceased to be. My guess is they had had sex and made up and all was well. (I would not have known this at twelve but, at sixteen, I could see how things worked out for a married couple.)

Joseph—that's the other me—got up in the morning and went to school as usual. In the schoolyard, he watched for Charlene to arrive. (I had almost forgotten about Charlene.) Charlene was happy to see me and I was happy to see her.

But back to real life. There *was* a girl named Charlene back then. Charlene called me Joey. We had started out as friends but I found myself with a crush on her. Charlene was a little cool to me at first, if memory serves me well, but I had cheered her up after her dog died and she started being nice to me.

Nice meant that we walked around outside the school together and traded sandwiches at lunch. I loaned her lunch money one day when she'd forgotten sandwiches, and I wouldn't let her pay me back.

And we'd hang out after school. I'd go to her house. She'd come over to mine. Sometimes we were alone in my house or hers. Our parents didn't seem to mind. Her parents liked me; my parents liked her. Charlene was smart, fun to talk to, and in a twelve-year-old sort of way, really cute. Other kids made fun of our "relationship." Oh, and did I mention she wore braces? Yes, she did. Her parents wanted her to have straight teeth.

After the accident, I was in a fog for a long while. (I can't say exactly how long—maybe the fog never fully lifted.) Charlene called me but I was not home. I'd been placed with some temporary foster parents. I called her but when she answered, I didn't know what to say so I just hung up. This happened more than once.

Here's the thing. We never actually had a chance to get back together after that. I got transferred to another school. I gave up trying to call her. She must have given up trying to get in touch with me.

But in my alternate time line where my parents just have a small argument but no accident, Charlene and Joey become loyal to each other—great friends who decide that what they have is more than a friendship. If twelve was too young to actually fall in love, thirteen was not. Thirteen was just right. And thirteen was just around the corner.

Now, if you are still following this little fairy tale, you will roll your eyes and say, "No way," out loud when I tell you that in this other time line they continue this relationship right through high school, through all the ups and downs of adolescent life, through all the stupid shit thrown at you when you are that age. They graduate and—get this—they get married.

I don't know what happens after that. I really don't. Do they have kids? Do they live happily ever after? (Does anyone live happily ever after?) Would they have even gotten together if Charlene's dog, a cocker spaniel named Ted, had not died?

What if all of this actually existed on some other time line? *I now pronounce you man and wife. I now give you a life.* What if it is actually happening now? Joey-1 is still with Charlene. They are not married yet but still in school. They are sixteen. Are they having sex? Is it really love? What if?

After the accident, though, Joey-1 probably ceased to exist. The Charlene thing ended. And Joseph woke up in the morning to this other life, his only life. The one where he is now sixteen, daydreaming his life away, certain that nothing makes sense and not expecting it to ever change. The boy is certainly not thinking about marriage and he is certainly not getting any sex.

And Charlene had faded entirely from his memory, from my memory. Until now.

In my mind, I saw her braces first, then I saw the rest of her. I remembered how sweet she was. How she liked it when I said nice things to her. (Joey was like that.)

And I guess that's when I heard the voice of Joey-1. "Find her, dude," he seemed to say. "Find her."

CHAPTER SIX

GLORIA WAS STILL DEPRESSED AGAIN IN SCHOOL TODAY. I FOUND HER staring into her open locker. "The arguments are getting worse," she said.

"What do they argue about?"

"Money," she said. "And me. My mom thinks there's something wrong with me."

"There's nothing wrong with you. You're perfect."

"I'm not perfect. My mom says she thinks I've got a serious problem. But then my dad yells at her and tells her to stop saying that. What should I do?"

"What can you do?"

"I don't know. I think that they're thinking of breaking up. And it's because of me. And I need to stop it from happening."

"Do you think you can do that?"

"I don't know. But I feel that it's all my fault."

Joey-1 had snuck up on me again. *That's how I felt*, he seemed to be saying inside my head. "It's not your fault," I said. But I didn't know if I was saying it to Gloria or saying it to me.

In biology class, we discussed a cheerful little theory devised by an English biologist (also an economist, I think) named Robert Malthus. Mrs. Godot called it the "Malthusian population theory." You recall how much I like theories, so I was quite alert and not drifting off to anywhere.

Bobby Malthus, who must have been a real wet blanket at parties, suggested that the number of people on earth would increase at a geometric rate but that the food supply (and other resources) would increase only moderately, or not at all. So, the more the population increased, the less food and everything else you'd have to keep everybody alive. The result would be massive poverty and starvation. The so-called "good news" is that there will be an almost automatic decrease in the population from disease, famine, high infant mortality rates, and—that good old standby used to reduce population down through the ages—war.

Malthus made a small suggestion that some of the nastiness could be offset by what was referred to as "moral restraint." Mrs. Godot thought that meant people being nice to each other and sharing what they had so everyone could live. Fat chance of that working. It also meant to stop having kids. Malthus probably thought this meant not having sex. His theory was published in 1798 when birth control was iffy at best. So he was maybe thinking that humans would stop having sex in order to save the world from pestilence, plagues, wars, and so forth. I can just imagine the morally restrained husbands of the world saying to their wives, "Honey, let's not do it tonight so that you won't get pregnant and the world will have one less mouth to feed and we'll avoid the deaths of thousands, if not millions." No, I can't see that happening.

But then I am a guy who has not had sex yet. What would I know about "moral restraint?" At least no one can blame me personally for the wars, the shortage of food globally, and the high infant mortality rate in Third World countries. The word for *not* doing something (like sex for example) is "abstinence," which my trusty two-volume *Oxford English Dictionary* defines as "the act of withholding." To abstain is to *not* do something. Abstain from sex, abstain from drinking, abstain from eating.

So once again, *not* doing something can have very positive results. Like the Buddhists say, "Don't just do something, sit there." Abstinence makes the heart grow fonder.

So me *not* having sex is probably good for something. I'm helping to save the world by not having sex today. Robert Malthus would be proud of me. Of course, he had his detractors. The ones who said that we are a smart and compassionate species and would not keep allowing our fellow man (woman and child) to die. Technology would come to our aid and we'd devise new and better ways to feed, house, and save everyone's ass. Everyone who has money, that is. Everyone who is not dirt poor.

I have this feeling that the other me, Joey-1, would have had sex by now. Possibly with Charlene if they'd still been together. Possibly with Rachelle Drummond in the school closet. Hey, maybe I would have turned out like Oliver Julian. Or not.

Gloria was not in my biology class and I had decided that a discussion of the Malthusian theory would not cheer her up. I didn't know what to do to help Gloria, but all that thinking about abstinence had made me a little weird. Fired up the hormones or something.

So between classes, I tracked Gloria down at her locker—she was staring into it again like there was someone there. I turned her around, took off her glasses, and I kissed her. No lie.

I kissed her and then waited for a response.

It was not a masterful kiss, I admit. It was a kind of kiss of dare. I had dared myself to kiss her. And almost wimped out. It was a kiss of desperation. I had to kiss someone. I could have done nothing, I know—my big kick of negative capability. "The less you do, the more good you will achieve." But I was in denial or in rebellion against dark forms of tyranny—like the French in 1798, rising up against oppression.

Exactly *why* did I kiss her? you (whoever you are) might wonder. I had never kissed her before. Most would even say she didn't look like a girl you'd kiss. She didn't look like a girl who *wanted* to be kissed. As previously noted, the world does not make sense. There is no discernible meaning. So it was a random kiss in a random universe. And people were watching.

Where had this idea come from? you might ask. What kind of freak am I? Thoughts about the death and dying of millions, a planet full of starving humans, talk of population decline, war and pestilence. Does that make a boy kiss a girl? I think not.

Instead, an idea to act in some small positive (and somewhat hormonally charged) way burst like a bubble in the brain of Joseph. Joey maybe coaching him. Time to make up for lost time, Mr. Joe-Seph. Maybe that.

At first, Gloria-In-Excelsis was shocked. And Joseph was shocked. And the other girls nearby at their lockers checking their cell phones, they were shocked too. And at least one boy grimaced. (Yes, I know a grimace when I see one.)

I was still holding G's glasses in my hand. My face was still close to Gloria's and I could feel her warm breath. I could see from her face that she had been crying—not much, but a small tear drop had, before the kiss, made its tiny stream down her face. And this close, frozen in time, it seemed, I realized she was even prettier than I had imagined. She was a beauty in hiding.

No, I did not kiss her a second time. At that point I didn't quite believe I had kissed her at all. But I had. The shock wave was wearing off. I didn't say anything. She didn't say anything. Probably because we had both lost the capacity for speech. The word "abstinence" appeared in my brain again. But I had already achieved the double negative. I had abstained from not kissing her.

She took a breath. I realized that both of us had stopped breathing. I took a breath.

And then she smiled.

She smiled and she hugged me. Me. A hug.

The bell rang, announcing that the next class was starting. Action in the hallway up to that point had frozen like one of those freeze-frame scenes in a movie. Now people came back to life and started moving. I heard one guy, walking by, say, "What the hell was that?" A girl said, "Man, this school is getting so weird."

Gloria did not appear self-conscious. She took her arms from around me and smiled some more. I had not seen her smile like this for a long time. Her eyes looked kind of soft and out of focus but that could have been because I was still holding her glasses.

A bit of the old me, Joseph, had re-established control of my brain. "I'm sorry," I said. Dumb thing to say for sure, but it came out.

"Don't be," she said. And then *she* kissed *me*.

And we were both late for class. Gloria's French teacher, Ms. Lalonde, was holding the door open to her nearby classroom. She was watching us and cleared her throat rather loudly in a French teacher sort of way. Gloria closed her locker and then touched my hand as she retrieved her glasses. She began to walk away, still smiling.

I wandered, stumbled really, off to my own class on the other side of the building. It took me a few minutes to remember what class I had next. Right. Math. Mr. Dexter announced as I walked in, "Joseph, you are late."

"Thank you," I said and took a seat near the window.

There is another theory about our world that suggests that for one person to be happy, someone must be equally unhappy somewhere else. It's kind of like Einstein's conservation of matter and energy thing. Only so much happiness to go around, so if it's doled out in one place, it's taken away somewhere else. If that is true, I apologize to the unknown person I made unhappy. But here at Northside Regional High, for a brief moment, I had taken away Gloria's pain. And I felt good about it. In a random universe, I was beginning to discover, there were certain illogical actions that could have very positive results.

CHAPTER SEVEN

HENRY AND CELIA.

The kiss must have triggered something. Can kissing do that? Unleash memories? It made me think of Charlene, sure. She was the first girl I ever kissed. But it got me thinking about my Bio-Mom and Bio-Dad too. They had kissed a lot. It was kind of embarrassing, really. No twelve-year-old kid wants his parents smooching in public. By the front door, in the driveway, in the mall. They would have smooched in the movie theater like teenagers if they'd made it that night.

When I got home from school, I unearthed the one photo album I have with pictures from back then. There's a box, too, with random photos somewhere, but the album was something that Will and Beth helped me put together when I moved in. They thought it would help.

I opened it and stared at a picture of my dad first. It was a photo of him before I had been born. He was in a rock band then. A heavy metal band called Jackhammer. "There were a lot of tool names going around for bands in those days," I remember Henry saying. "The Drill, Wrench, Rip Saw, Chisel, that sort of thing." My dad's hair was long and hanging down in front of his face in the photo. He held his guitar, slung low in front of him. It was a pose. Jackhammer had recorded some music, "on our own dime," as he put it. They played some clubs and toured—well, at least they had some gigs out of town.

That's how he met my mom. No kidding. Celia had just started teaching elementary school. Celia had that dark black hair and a really nice way of smiling. One of her friends had invited her out on a Friday to hear some "music." Celia thought her friend meant a different kind of music. Something easy on the ears. She thought it would be folk music or maybe folk-rock. Instead, she found herself staring at a rude-looking and rude-talking heavy metal band playing loud, angry metal. "I hated it at first," she had told me. "I mean, who would name a band Jackhammer? And why did they have to be so loud? But then the band took a break and he came over to the table." The *he* was, of course, my future father.

Henry reportedly sat down and just stared at my mother through the long straggly hair that hung down in front of his face. "He spooked me at first," I remember Mom saying. "Just staring like that. My friend, Kathleen, got up to go to the bathroom. And I was left there alone with this freaky guy who said nothing, just stared."

So you can see that I came by my nerdy weirdness honestly. My father's genes. I think I'm only now beginning to see how I am my father's son.

"Henry," he had finally said, by way of belated introduction. He shot his hand out to shake. But he did it so fast and so aggressively that my mom jumped.

"Celia," she finally said and shook his hand. Henry continued to stare at her and later reported that her dark hair and large dark eyes reminded him of a seal. In a good way. He had always thought seals were very beautiful. Their faces, at least.

They did not kiss that night, according to the legendary story. Instead, they engaged in awkward conversation that I imagine went something like this.

"So, you're in a band?" she said.

"Yes, I am. And you?"

"I teach in an elementary school."

"No, I mean really?" he would have said.

"Really. I teach nine- and ten-year-olds."

"Wow. What do you teach them?"

"How to spell. Arithmetic. Social skills."

"Social skills? They do that in school now?"

"Yes. We're big on conflict resolution."

Conflict resolution is a term Seal liked to use around the house. I always thought it should be applied to stopping wars, resolving hostile differences between nations, and that sort of thing. "It does," she had explained to me. "But you have to teach people the skills when they are young. If you can resolve a conflict in the schoolyard, you can prevent a war."

So my mom was in charge of preventing World War Three. "There's not a bully out there that I can't learn to like," I remember her saying. "People are inherently good. Sometimes you just have to bring it out of them." My mom said stuff like that all the time. I feel bad that I sometimes laughed at her. I thought I knew more about bullies than she did. I'd seen a few rotten ones in my twelve years and it was hard to see the "good" in them. I rolled my eyes at her but my dad would furtively shake his head and make a secretive wave of his hand, coaching me to be nice to my mother. Later he'd say, "Be nice to your mother."

On that fateful night when my parents met, the conversation was awkward, for sure. The band's break was almost over and my dad gave it his best shot. "I'm gonna play a love song I wrote for you. I didn't know I wrote it for you. I didn't have anybody to play it for, but now I want to play it for you."

My mom blushed, I am sure, as only an elementary teacher can blush.

Later she would report to me, "It didn't sound like any love song I'd ever heard. It was loud and raunchy and I couldn't understand any of the words. But I was smitten."

Smitten. That was the word she used. "Inspired or inflamed with love," so says my trustworthy *OED*.

They were as different as two people could be. Dad wanted to be the next Ozzie Osborne. Mom wanted to teach little children to be good citizens. But they were both smitten. If they had been more cautious, I would not have come into this world. Like many before me, I was an accident. I'm sure there is a more complete story but it would have been revealed to me later in life, not before twelve. All I know is that I was not intended.

So even unmarried elementary school teachers sometimes have sex with long straggly-haired metal guitarists in bands named after tools. It's a strange world indeed. And I am the product of that world and of that most human but most unlikely union of a man and a woman.

When news reached Henry that Seal was "with child," Henry cried. But he cried in a good way. "I was so happy," he said, "but I was afraid she would push me away. I was pretty insecure. Most lead singers in metal bands were insecure in those days. And assholes. Most of us were assholes. We just didn't know it."

My father used that kind of language around me even when I was young. I remember that now.

The other photo right beside my hairy dad was Mom at around the same time. Funny, there were no photos here of the two of them together—no photos of them *before* my father cut his hair, at least. Lots of them together *after* she scissored his locks. But my mom, the Seal, was young in the solo picture and gorgeous. I would have fallen in love with her if I had been my father or any other member of Jackhammer. But I guess that's a kind of weird thing for me to say.

The other guys in the band truly wanted to go on the road. There was this great dream to "hit the Coast." The Coast was where it was happening, where Jackhammer might have broken through the concrete wall that was keeping them from stardom. "But I couldn't leave Seal," my dad said in one of his many tellings of the tale. "I couldn't leave you."

So he split from the band, with a lot of hard feelings and very little conflict resolution. And he asked Seal to cut his hair. Celia said he didn't have to, but he thought he had to do it "to fit into the daytime world," as he called it. And he got a job at a hardware store. They moved into an apartment that smelled like cat pee and had the world's loudest refrigerator. As I gathered together my energy to come into this world, my mom took a leave from work, my dad worked overtime, and then there were three.

Not long after Joey-1 appeared on the scene, they got married.

And the rest, as they say, is history. I sucked milk, burped, vomited, dirtied a lot of diapers, and eventually discovered there was a world out there to be explored. My dad was offered a job representing a power tool company. He became a salesman of sorts but didn't have to travel very far from home and never had to stay away overnight. He made better money than at the hardware store so they could move into a nicer apartment, without cat pee smell and with a quiet refrigerator.

And he dreamed of one day going back to playing music. I still have his old dented and dinged Fender Strat here in my closet. He used to play it sometimes on Saturdays after we had moved again, this time into the house. He started teaching me to play the guitar when I was nine, but I was a slow learner and my fingers were kind of small. "If I can play the guitar, then you can play the guitar," he said, even as I struggled to form a basic G chord. Pretty soon I had the G and I could play the opening part to "Smoke on the Water" by an old band called Deep Purple.

My mom didn't go back to teaching until I was six. But when she did, she picked right back up on the conflict resolution thing and taught her kids how to use "I messages"— ways of speaking in a disagreement where there is no blame placed on the other person. "I understand you are feeling angry, Joey, but you still can't eat all that candy." That sort of thing. "You messages" were out. "I messages" were in.

It should have been a happily-ever-after story, don't you think? Metalhead meets his Madonna. (Not *the* Madonna.)

So you must be wondering what it is like to suddenly reminisce like this, reflect on my old life, the one that's shattered and gone. Well, it seems as if none of it could be real. So I close the album and put it away. It's gonna take a lifetime to fit those pieces back into my life. There were no grandparents to take me in. All of them were dead. And there were no kindly aunts and uncles. There were social workers and a couple of foster homes. A damn good lawyer and then Will and Beth stepped up to the plate. No kids of their own and willing to adopt a traumatized twelve-year-old who, according to the shrinks, might act out with his hurt or anger in any number of bizarre or violent ways.

But they took me anyway. And I could not figure out who or what I should get angry at. Except me, of course. Textbook case. I blamed me for the death of the rock star and the teacher-goddess.

But I think I eased up on the blame when I came to the brilliant conclusion that the world did not make any sense. None at all. And that helped a little. It eased the burden of living.

CHAPTER EIGHT

THE WORD "TRAGEDY" HAS ITS ROOTS IN ANCIENT GREEK APPARENTLY, where it originally meant "a male goat." That doesn't seem to make a lot of sense today, but then, what does make sense? My old *OED* (bought by my first mother years ago at a library book sale, by the way) tells me that a tragedy is "a play or other literary work of a serious or sorrowful character with a fatal or disastrous conclusion." Maybe because goats were sacrificed to the gods in ancient Greece—at least, that's what I'm thinking—but it could be something else.

"Fatal" is another of one those intriguing words. Traditionally meaning "doomed" or "decreed by fate: inevitable, necessary." Today, we use it rather loosely, of course, but it always implies a bad thing. The Romans had three goddesses of human fate. They were in charge of making up the rules of what happens to whom and when. Their names were Clotho, Lachesis, and Atropos. Three females who said: good stuff for this kid, rotten luck for buddy.

It was my first mother who got me interested in words. Words lead to ideas and sometimes ideas prompt me to stop thinking about my own grief. I wish sometimes I could blame Clotho, Lachesis, and Atropos for what they did, but I don't think they exist. I don't believe in Roman or Greek gods. Those gods did some pretty freaky stuff and because they were gods, they got away with a lot of it. So what do you suppose happened to those gods, once people stopped believing in them?

Now, about God, the God with the capital G, please don't ask me if I believe in him. Because I would simply be silent. I would not give you an answer.

◀ ■ ▶

Well, sorry I had to cut that last session short. I grew weary of thinking about goddesses, fate, fatalities, fatalism, or any of it. I wanted my mind to settle down and go blank. So I shut off the recorder and I stared out the window. I stared at a tree in the yard. There was a squirrel in that tree and I wished my fate had been to be that squirrel, not Joseph, sitting in his bedroom alone.

What happened to me then was this. I felt a heaviness sneaking up from the back of my brain. The heaviness made me panic at first, but then a dark, warm, empty feeling flooded into me.

I went to sleep after that and woke up still feeling heavy. Drugged even. I had been dreaming—something from back before the accident. It was fuzzy but one thing was clear. For the first time in a really long while—four years maybe— I wanted to go back to my old hometown. I wanted to go back to Riverside, the town I'd lived in up until I was twelve years old.

But I didn't have the courage to do it on my own.

So I called Gloria. Every now and then, my mind slipped back to the memory of the two of us kissing and I had made many mental notes that we should do more of that soon.

"Hello?" she said. She sounded strangely lifeless.

"You okay?" I asked.

"I can't seem to snap out of it. I just feel like sleeping."

"I think I know a little bit about how you feel. Something happened to me today. I don't know what it was. But it freaked me out." I explained to her my weird little blip.

"Yeah, I feel the heaviness, too. But it doesn't seem to go away."

"But will you help me? I can't do this alone."

"Help you do what?"

"Reconnect. I've shut out everything of the past for so long that none of it seems real. I can't remember a lot of things. But now I need to know."

"I don't know if I can do anything."

"Please?" I begged.

She sighed. "Sure. Where do we start?"

"Would you help me locate Charlene?"

"Your girlfriend from when you were twelve?" She sounded a little miffed.

"Is that too weird?"

"Yes," she said emphatically.

"For some reason, I need to start with her."

"Why?"

"I don't know. I guess because she was my first girlfriend," I said. And I almost said, "and my last." But I didn't. Like I said, Gloria wasn't exactly my girlfriend. She was my friend.

Gloria let out another sigh. "What was her last name?"

"Thomas. Charlene Thomas."

"And you really want me to find her."

"Charlene Thomas, now sixteen, I presume, lives in Riverside, goes to Riverside High, I would guess."

"And you want me to contact her and tell her you'd like to meet her?"

"Yes."

There was a pause and then Gloria said, "I'll see what I can do." And then hung up.

I sat by the window again, staring out at the tree, the big oak tree that the birds liked—sparrows and grackles and robins and catbirds. And blue jays. In my next life, if there was a next life, I wanted to come back as a blue jay. When things got bad, you could just fly away. And blue jays had a really cool look and attitude.

Why did I want to see Charlene? I hadn't spoken to her or had contact with her since my parents died. It had something to do with the way I felt for her. I had never felt that way again. I had had a crush on that girl that was so bad. And she had liked me—in a twelve-year-old girl sort of way. But it was pretty heavy back then. Back then, I woke up in the morning and I couldn't wait to get to school—so I could see her. So I could talk to her and look in her eyes. When you are love-struck as a twelve-year-old boy, you are positively gooney. But what was I doing now?

What I was doing now was waiting for my best and only friend Gloria—a girl who maybe was becoming much more than just a friend, a girl whose parents were about to break up, a girl possibly suffering from true depression—to find my old girlfriend. Was I crazy or what? I tried playing a video game but I couldn't concentrate. I checked my e-mail but there was only junk.

My mom yelled up and said it was time for dinner. I wasn't hungry but I always ate dinner with my parents. It was about the only time of day we were all together. And my father would freak if he thought I wasn't watching my nutrition. My guess is that it would be Indian food—it was my dad's night to cook. There would be curry for sure.

And then the phone rang. I saw that it was Gloria so I picked it up. "I found her," she said. "The Internet made it almost too easy. I still don't see why you asked *me* to do this for you. I feel like such a ... pimp."

Ouch. I'd never heard Gloria use that word before. And I could see that she was downright pissed at me. I pretended not to notice. "What did she say?"

"She seemed to think it was a little strange. As do I."

"But?"

"But she's willing to meet you. Tomorrow at her school. Three-thirty out in front by the buses. You really want to do this?"

"I don't know why. But yes."

"Good luck, then." Gloria was about to hang up. She was mad at me. She was jealous. I didn't quite know what to do with that.

"But I can't do it alone. You have to come with me."

"To meet your old girlfriend?"

"Yes."

"No way."

"If you do this for me, I'll do anything you ask me to do." I was desperate. It was a totally generic "anything" but I meant it. Gloria had never asked me to *do* anything special for her. She was so undemanding. I think that was part of why I liked her so much as a friend.

"Anything?"

"Sure."

"Okay. Then we have a deal."

◀ ■ ▶

I guess you'd like to know how that reunion worked out. So I'll pick up the tale from where I left off. I was nervous through the school day. Gloria acted kind of cool toward me and that was new. But she seemed to have broken out of her blues. "How are your parents doing?" I asked.

"They've stopped speaking to each other. It's very quiet around the house. And they don't sleep together anymore."

"That's a bad sign."

"Used to be they'd argue but they still went to bed together. But not anymore."

"I'm sorry."

"It's the way it goes," she said.

Gloria had done a little research to figure out how to get to Riverside by bus. We'd have to split from school early to make it there by three-thirty. It would have only been a twenty-minute ride in a car but it took an hour by bus, with one transfer.

On the bus, everyone looked bored. I was feeling kind of scared but tried not to show it. I still didn't know why I was doing this. And why was I doing this *now*? And what would I do once I got there?

"How often have you been back to Riverside since you moved in with Will and Beth?"

"Never," I admitted.

"Not once?"

"I've driven through here with my parents but even then, I never looked at anything. I pretended I'd never lived there."

"You were protecting yourself."

"What do you mean?"

"If you remembered, it would hurt badly. So you shut it out. I think I understand about shutting things out. But I've never experienced what you went through."

She was right. There was a lot I had shut out. Big chunks of my past I could not recall. I had found that I could get on with my life if I just shut out a lot of things.

"We're here," Gloria said, pointing out the window to Riverside High. I felt a cold chill go through me. I sat motionless. Gloria noticed this, took my hand, and led me down the aisle of the bus.

She was still holding my hand as we walked across the street to the school. I had not attended this school, of course, and I don't recall even seeing it, although I must have gone past here as a kid and looked at the building, thinking someday I'd be a big kid and go there. But now it all felt like unknown territory to me.

Most of the kids were hurrying off—some getting on buses, some walking. A couple of girls were sitting on a low stone wall chatting and some guys were patting pockets, looking for cigarettes. I looked for someone I thought could be Charlene, tried to picture her when she was twelve, tried to imagine what she might look like.

Gloria spotted her before me. Exactly how she knew it was her, I don't know. Maybe she'd found a photo on the Internet, maybe not.

"Charlene?" Gloria asked a girl—a very old-looking girl, a

very good-looking girl, that I would have assumed could *not* be Charlene.

The girl scowled at Gloria, then gave me the once-over. "Joey?"

I nodded. The young woman in front of me resembled nothing I could remember of the Charlene I knew. She was beautiful like a Rachelle Drummond, but hard-looking like Rachelle also. The kind of girl who would not even look at me in my high school and would not ever talk to me.

"I'm Gloria," Gloria said. "Joseph asked me to come along."

Charlene looked me over again, like she was examining a piece of gum stuck to her shoe. "What's this about, anyway?" she asked.

"I'm not sure," I said with as much courage as I could muster. "I'm trying to fit some pieces together."

"This has to do with your parents, right?" Charlene asked in a rather cold voice.

"I think so," I said.

Charlene looked a little nervous, like she wished she had not said yes to the meeting. "Can we go over there?" she asked, pointing to a park next to the school. "I need a smoke and I can't do it here on school grounds."

"Sure." So we walked to a picnic table and Charlene sat down on it. She fished for cigarettes in her purse and lit one. She didn't offer any to Gloria or me. She took a drag and re-laxed slightly but now looked away, not at me. I realized that she and I were so totally different that it was hard to believe that she had ever been my girlfriend, my first girlfriend.

All three of us were sitting on the table. We were all un-comfortable. Gloria was quiet now and Charlene was taking quick drags from her cigarette. "Do you remember much about us?" I asked.

"It was a long time ago, Joey. We were just kids."

"I know. But I have this feeling there was something unfinished."

She let out a cynical laugh. "Kind of a funny way of putting it."

I didn't know what to say next.

Charlene seemed even more agitated. "Look, I'm sorry about what happened to your parents. We all felt bad about that. It kind of shook us all up. Like it could have been any of our parents. And I had decided I'd do anything to help."

"I can't remember much about then," I said. "A lot of it is just a blank. Can you tell me something about what happened after the accident?"

"Not really. You just disappeared. I tried calling you but you never returned my calls. I tried going to your house but you weren't there. You just disappeared and never came back. Never phoned, never wrote. Not one word."

"I guess I didn't know what to do. I was only twelve."

"Yeah," she said, "Well, so was I." She seemed angrier now and I didn't get it.

I tried to change the subject. "So, like, tell me something about yourself—now."

Charlene stubbed out her cigarette on the top of the picnic table. "Look, Joey, Joseph, or whatever you call yourself now, I'd like to help you with your little therapy session but I don't think I'm up for it. I've got a life and maybe you need to get one, too. I was hurt when I never heard from you, okay? Even though it was you who lost your parents. I could not believe you never contacted me again. But I'll be honest, I got over it. I'm not sure why I agreed to meet with you now. Just curious, I guess. But I don't have much more to tell you. I think you better just take your nerdy little girlfriend here and go back to wherever you came from."

Gloria was staring at Charlene as she was standing up. Gloria only had one word for her. "Bitch," she said, loud enough for other people in the park to turn our way. Charlene glared at her but said nothing. And then she walked away.

CHAPTER NINE

"WELL, THAT WENT WELL," GLORIA SAID AFTER CHARLENE HAD stormed off.

I didn't know what to say. I was shell-shocked. I'd never seen Gloria get angry before. But I was thinking, maybe angry is better than depressed.

"I think she has issues," I said, referring to Charlene.

"Well, next time you want to track down old girlfriends, leave me out of it." Now she was mad at me.

"No more old girlfriends to track down. I think we should go home."

It took Gloria and me an hour to find the bus that would get us back home. Once we found a seat, Gloria seemed to calm down a bit. She leaned against the window at first and then leaned the other way against me, putting her head on my shoulder. I bent down and kissed her on the top of her head. She squirmed in a funny way that made me think she liked it. And I started to think about Gloria in a whole new way.

◄ ■ ►

Dean called to tell me that he read somewhere that you could cure anything with magnets. "So I bought some at the Dollar Store. I've got eight of them taped to my head right now."

"Is it working? How does it make you feel?"

"I feel a little light-headed. I think it must be working. But if I get too close to my TV, the picture goes funny."

"From the magnets," I said.

"Oh, right."

"Why do you think you need to put magnets on your head?" I asked.

"I'm trying to fix whatever is wrong with me."

"There's nothing wrong with you," I said.

"Well, do you think the magnets will work? Do you think they might make me smarter or anything?"

"Yes, I think they will work. Where'd you get the idea from?"

"A site on the Internet. A French dude named Mesmer came up with the concept a long time ago."

"Well, then, I'm sure it will make you smarter."

"Thanks, dude. See ya."

"See ya."

You can see why I worried about Dean. Dean was out there. And what was it with all the French? Wasn't Mesmer someone who pioneered hypnosis? Could magnets really change your mind or your body? Anything and everything can change your mind or body, I suppose.

So what am I to make of my meeting today with Charlene? People change. My tracking her down scared her. Scared me. Pissed Gloria right off. Some kind of lesson there. I think I'm getting a headache. I wonder if my mom has any Dollar Store magnets.

◄ ■ ►

Primordial soup. That's where we come from. Way back.

The earth was this big steaming watery sphere and that's where life started. In this broth, some chemicals randomly (or not) combined and bacteria was formed. The bacteria eventually evolved into you and me and learned to play video games and figured out how to cheat on taxes and parallel park a car. I'm leaving out a few steps along the evolutionary pathway, but you get the picture. A lot of missteps occurred along the way, of course. Many tragedies and some really funny stuff.

In the 1860s, others like me who were wondering about the various steps up from the basement of our origins wondered what our human ancestors were like. Were there families and monogamy or was that relatively modern? One lawyer-anthropologist (and there's a real career combo) named J.J. Bachofen suggested that at some point along the human road to civilization, there existed what he called "primitive promiscuity." This, I guess, is quite possible. No marriage licenses, no church ceremonies, no annoying uncles and aunts getting drunk at the wedding party and falling into the cake. Pairings were rather random and unregulated, and then there were babies. These were our ancestors. It must have been some wild times back there near the roots of the old family tree. Primordial soup to primitive promiscuity to this very confusing world we live in today.

This reminds me that I am cut off from my biological roots. I am the result of Henry and Seal. Jackhammer Jack and Pacifist Seal combined to create me. And only me. No brothers. No sisters. In one sense, I am all that is left of them except for those photos and the Fender Strat and possibly some grown-up kids out there who had my mom for a teacher and are refusing to fight in wars.

What if I hold in my head for just a minute that I am here on this planet for a purpose? Up, out of the soup and scandalous ancient sex, and descended from generations of Euro-white trash, no doubt, created by a rather wonderful pair of humans, and presented to the waiting world. Here I am. Here to do what?

Graduate high school and be emptied like yesterday's trash out into the great vacuum of the modern world. That's the only purpose I can see. And so, that makes me expendable.

The oddest thing of all about the death of my parents was this: the world continued on. It really did. It continued on more or less as if nothing happened. The sun came up. Buses ran on schedule. Someone took over my mom's teaching job. Someone else was hired to sell power tools. The vacuum filled.

◄ ■ ►

Today I discovered why Dean was hoping to fix himself with magnets.

The cyber bullies are after him. Oh, God. Did we truly ever evolve beyond poking each other with sticks, cannibalism, and tribal hatred? I think not. There is a video clip taken by someone's cell phone of Dean stuttering a wrong answer to a teacher's question in health class. It makes him look really stupid. There is a laugh track at the end of it. And people on the site have posted comments about him. All insulting. Not just kids from school. That's the kicker here. People from all over. Making fun of him. Saying cruel things—really cruel things.

The worst one was this: "This human piece of crap should not be allowed to live." Posted anonymously, of course. Who would do such a thing?

Dean told me about this during third period. I cut class and we hung out in the library. The librarian, Ms. Gray, said we could stay there. She understood Dean. She could see he was hurting.

"Just ignore it and it will go away," I told Dean.

"Why me? Why did they pick me?"

"I don't know. I don't think they cared who it was. They just made you the victim."

"My mom says I should go to the principal and tell him."

"Nah. I think that will only draw more attention to it."

"Kids look at me in the hall. They laugh at me."

"I know what that feels like," I said.

"So?"

"So do nothing."

"Nothing?"

"Yeah. Nothing. Head high. Eyes straight ahead. Forget about the magnets."

"You didn't tell anyone about the magnets?"

"No, I didn't. Besides, I think you're onto something. In my father's store, they sell inserts for your shoes. Guess what's in the inserts?"

"Magnets."

"Yep. My father's not convinced, but some people buy them and say it cures their aching feet."

"I feel a little better."

"Good. Was it me or the magnets?"

"A little of both, I think."

"Dean, when you and I are thirty, I want the two of us to climb a really high mountain."

His face lit up. "Like Everest?"

"No. Something smaller. Something manageable."

"That would be sweet."

◀ ■ ▶

Dean will one day be a very important person. The pain of his youth, cyber bullying included, will fuel him to save the shrimp and salmon, and possibly rid the world of deadly floating fishnets that kill untold numbers of fish. He will move on from trying to improve himself with taped magnets and probably kick some serious ass in the intellectual world. I know this, or at least, I believe this. And I wonder what the difference is between knowing and believing.

Gloria is getting over being angry at me. "I was jealous, you know," she told me.

"Why would you be jealous?"

She gave me a look.

"Oh, the bitch, you mean?"

"Yes. Her."

"That whole scene wasn't what I expected."

"What did you expect?"

"Some clues. About then. About me back then. About who I was."

"Do you think you learned anything?"

"No. Not from Charlene. But I think I have to go back to Riverside again. There's this big hole in my life."

"Maybe it's better to live in the present than in the past."

"Does that work for you?"

She looked less sure of herself now. "No. Not really. The past was not so bad for me. Back when my parents got along.

The present is not so good."

"What can I do to help?" I asked.

"Make the world go away."

I flicked my hands out in opposite directions in the air. "Phht," I said. "Gone."

Gloria smiled and what was left of the world, a small little cocoon around us, became very bright. And there was a sound track. A single, surging chord that sounded like it came from my father's electric guitar plugged into his big old Marshall amp with the stacked speakers.

CHAPTER TEN

I AM ALONE WITH MY DIGITAL RECORDER RIGHT NOW IN THE FOREST and it is spring. I have nothing really to say or report, so don't expect this to "go anywhere." Just some random thoughts.

There are birds in the trees. I'm glad this planet has birds. They sing and caw and make strange noises. Some are pleasant, some not. If I can't think of anything else to be and if I fail at managing a health food store, I may become an ornithologist. Spend my life studying birds. Do some people actually get paid for this?

Someone phones you up to go bowling and you say, "I'm sorry, I can't go bowling today. I'm flying to Zanzibar to study the white-breasted gumple bird." I made that bird up, sorry. Don't know what birds fly around Zanzibar but I will find out.

Or you are at a party. I mean, I am at a party and I am twenty-nine and still kind of nerdy, but women find me attractive. This is fantasy, I know, but it's my fantasy. And I'm drinking ... what am I drinking? I'm drinking a glass of red Chilean wine. No, I can't see that. I am drinking a beer imported from Holland. Okay. And a very attractive woman with an accent (Dutch, French, Czech?) sidles up to me and asks what I do for a living. "I'm an ornithologist," I say. "My research concerns the mating habits of the finches." And she becomes very interested in me. We have a totally hot thing that develops and she says she wants to fly to Zanzibar with me. So we ditch the party and fly to Zanzibar.

Suppose my life goes like that? It could, I know. I'm not ruling anything out. In a random universe, anything can happen.

I read somewhere that civilizations destroy themselves quite quickly (relatively speaking) as soon as they reach a technological stage of creating weapons of mass destruction. As you may know, we have already reached that stage. On other planets, as you might probably guess, civilizations have come and gone once they figured out how to set off theta-radiation bombs or time collapsers or mass media mind-melters or what have you. We have our arsenals of nuclear, biological, and chemical weapons. A touch of plutonium can go a long way, they say. Release some into the atmosphere and wipe out millions.

I have yet to learn how to mourn for my parents. How does a person mourn for the death of millions? Or the death of everyone on the planet. Who does the eulogy? Who sends flowers and Hallmark cards? Who inherits what?

The meek, according to the Bible, will inherit the earth. I've read the Bible, on my own, without the churches or Sunday schools. Maybe the mind-melting gases end up killing off everyone but the meek. People like Dean. Nothing left of human life on earth but Deanworld. And birds. I want the birds to survive. Crows, blue jays, cardinals, sparrows, finches, penguins, puffins, magpies, whiskey jays, juncos, swallows, doves (in the meekful Deanworld, there will be a plethora of doves), and ducks. A world of ducks without hunters.

◀ ■ ▶

I am back. Further into the forest now. I stopped to pee on a plant and hope that my urine will be nourishing for it. It was some kind of fern. Very ancient in design, I believe, and very cool. I am not following any trail now but just randomly walking and talking about whatever comes into my head. Will recently gave me a little pep talk about digital diary talking, said that I should "let it flow."

So I am in the pathless forest. It's not big enough to really get lost in and there is trash here and there, signs that others have come here to—do what? The evidence suggests drink beer. Drink coffee from paper cups. Eat hamburgers? Smoke cigarettes. Have sex. Yes, there were at least two condoms. So maybe it was sequential over a long period of time or maybe someone, possibly even someone from my own school, a guy with a weird plan, said to his girlfriend, "Hey, I have an idea. Let's go out in the woods and have a beer, then drink some coffee from Tim Hortons, eat a couple of Wendy's hamburgers, smoke cigarettes, and then have sex." And presumably, according to this scenario, the young willing female said, "Wow. Cool. What a great idea."

If that really happened, then there probably is no hope for the human race.

Moving on now. Walking through very tall ferns that have not been pissed on by me. The trees—oak, I think, and maple—are tall here. I am beneath their canopy. I feel protected. It is a warm day, but not hot. Everything is green. Green is good. Remind me that if we destroy earth and I am left all alone in a runaway space capsule and God presents himself in the form of a small stowaway dove and God asks me to invent a new planet, remind me to say I want lots of greens and blues. Blue sky. Green leaves. My hope would be that God-the-dove would not reply, "It's been done before." No, if some things were lost, we'd have to figure out how to create them again. Re-creation. Not recreation. But it's funny that it is spelled that way.

I stop to touch the rough bark of an oak tree and notice that there is a small highway of ants going up and down. I don't think ants are as annoying as most people think. I rather like ants with all that energy and ambition. One is carrying a leaf that is three times larger than he is. An ant with ambition.

Some say I lack ambition. That I haven't found my "purpose in life" yet. When your parents die at twelve, it really throws you off. Not that I had a purpose back then. I just had a life that sort of made sense. Mom. Dad. A bike. I really liked riding that bike on the sidewalks. A sled. Favorite TV shows. Did I ever tell you that I get physically ill if certain rerun TV shows come on? I do and I know why and I steer way clear of them. I won't name them. I can't even do that without nausea. But then, I suppose, I am not the first or last person to be nauseated by television. I read in the paper that the viewers of television are on the decline. Could this possibly be because the quality of TV programs is so bad? But this is not a rant about TV.

I'd prefer an oak tree to a TV any day. An oak tree would make an excellent companion. Quiet. Dependable. Unwilling to gossip or get involved in cyber bullying. Allowing ants to crawl from forest floor to sky. Producing leaves and helping to create oxygen. Imagine having a friend who could do photosynthesis. At the proverbial party, introducing him.

"Hi, this is my friend Oaky. He can convert sunlight into energy and, instead of farting, he gives off oxygen. He's got great roots and lots of strong limbs. And he never complains or makes annoying comments."

Oaky, thanks for letting me hang with you for a while. Time to move on.

◄ ■ ►

In fairy tales, people get lost in forests. Then good or bad things happen to them. Right now, you could probably say I am lost. Sort of. I don't really know the way back but I am confident that if I keep walking, I will come out somewhere. This is not the Northwest Territories or anything, where if you got lost and decided to walk in one of several perfectly wrong directions, you'd hike maybe a thousand miles before you bumped back into civilization. No, this is not like that. This forest has been whittled down and, in my lifetime, may even be gone, I am sad to say.

Did it ever occur to you that we are all headed in the wrong direction? Civilization, I mean. We are kind of like *in* the Northwest Territories and have said, I think I'll walk in *that* direction. And it's the wrong one. Hah. Sometimes I think we are all lost. Not just me.

There's no trash in this part of the forest and the trees are closer together. The leaves above keep out the sun. It is womb-like here and I sit down on a cushion of star moss that is very soft and welcoming. I allow my mind to clear and grow peaceful. My voice, as I speak, seems to be coming from somewhere else, not from me, but I find that rather interesting as well.

What I'm feeling, I suppose, is rather primitive. This is what people used to feel in a forest. Native people, older people. The forest as home, as sanctuary. This feels so different from school or sitting in front of a computer. I realize now I am looking for something here. And I've found something but it's not easy to explain.

I feel connected. That's it.

Connected. A good word if ever there was one. Because when I was twelve, once I'd lost them, I felt totally disconnected. And part of me has ever since. But there is a thread to things ...

A thread. A thread to things? Where did that come from? That's one of the funny things about me. Despite my beliefs, I keep *trying* to connect things. I keep trying to have things make sense. This happens when I let my guard down. Like now.

And I know this is all gibberish and, if you are listening, you are wondering if it is time to just give up on me. Am I insane? Am I just blathering? Is this going anywhere?

The answers are Yes, Yes, and No. So there. Shoot me.

◄ ■ ►

When a tree dies in a forest, it eventually falls over and starts to rot. Moss and fungus and ferns and other plants start to grow on it—along its trunks and limbs where it has fallen. After a while, you can't see the rotting wood of the tree, just the outline of the tree in the plant life it is sustaining. How cool is that? In dying, you aid in the growth of other life. What a grand idea. It would be nice if humans could do that in some form or other. I'm being philosophical here. I don't just mean plant a watermelon on my grave, because we all know that when you die, you get pumped with chemicals that preserve you. But preserve you for what?

No, I mean that when you die, maybe you leave some meaning behind. Your life has meant something that other people can build on. Some beautiful thing. Some life-sustaining thing. Maybe I should start my own religion.

But I'm not that ambitious.

◄ ■ ►

By now, you will have noticed how positive the influence of the forest is on me: birds, ferns, trees, ants, mosses. They do seem to have something to teach. I almost wish that Gloria was here to share this ... whatever this is.

But then I wouldn't be alone and it's the alone thing, here in the woods, that is putting me in a good place. Like the doctor gave me the following prescription: "Take two hours in the forest and call me in the morning."

My guess is that it is three o'clock in the afternoon. A Saturday afternoon. Ever notice that we have names for everything? Even days of the week. Times of day. The past, present, and future. We have a habit of dividing things up into little parcels and then naming them. If we name a thing, does that give it meaning?

Now, you have to keep in mind that, right now, I am a boy in a forest speaking into a digital recorder. If there was anyone else out here—and there may well be, but I can't see them—they would, of course, hear me rambling on with all that I have said to myself. And I would be considered by them as a lunatic and they would carve a wide berth around me. They might report to the police about a crazed teenage boy talking to himself in the forest. Some might think me dangerous.

And I may well be talking to myself since there is no real guarantee that anyone will actually listen to this. That's part of what gives me the freedom to explore. That single perfect person, my prime audience, may never hear it. It may all be an exercise in absurdity. It may mean nothing at all.

But I will not give up my mission—which is to explore the random universe.

At this moment—and I know it will not last—I like where I am. I like what I am doing. I like who I am and I have released myself from the past and the future.

For the moment, for the time being, I have set myself free.

I think the word for that is emancipation.

CHAPTER ELEVEN

MY CELL PHONE RINGS. IT'S 11:30 AT NIGHT. IT'S GLORIA. "MY DAD JUST left," she says. "They had another argument about me."

"I'm so sorry," I say, not really knowing what to say.

"I tried to talk to my mom but she was so angry. She locked herself in her bedroom. I don't know what to do."

I could tell Gloria was in panic mode. "Do you want me to come over?" I had never done such a thing in my life, but Gloria seemed desperate.

"No. I don't want to be in this house right now. I just want to go ... somewhere." Her voice trailed off. I didn't like the sound of it.

"Come here, then," I said. It was not at all like me to take charge.

"I'm scared."

I thought about Gloria out there in the dark, walking more than twenty blocks to get here. "I'll wake my dad. We'll drive over and pick you up."

"Will you do that?"

"Yes. He'll understand."

"Are you sure?"

I wasn't sure at all. This would freak out my father. Both my parents would think they were intruding on someone else's personal family affairs. "Yes. Hang tight. We'll be over. Write a note and leave it for your mother. Tell her you are okay. Tell her you were scared and leave our phone number."

There were a few seconds of silence. "Are you sure?"

"Yes," I said.

"Okay."

◄ ■ ►

I knocked on my parents' bedroom door and my mother mumbled something, so I opened the door and stepped in. It was dark.

"It's Gloria," I said. "She needs a place to stay tonight."

"Why? What happened?" my mom asked.

"Parents had a fight. Her dad left."

"Shouldn't she be there with her mother?" Mom asked.

"Um ... I think she's scared. She's been depressed."

"Might not be so good to get involved," Dad said.

"She needs me," I said.

"Oh," he replied.

"Dad, can you drive me?"

My mom started to say something like, "Are you sure?" but Dad was already out of bed. "I'll get my clothes."

◄ ■ ►

Gloria had the porch light on and was standing inside the door when we pulled up in her driveway. As soon as she saw us, she was out of the house and walking toward us. I got out of the front seat, opened the back door, and got in the back seat with her. My dad stayed perfectly silent.

I held her hand on the drive back. She said, "Thanks for coming," but then fell silent.

When we arrived home, my mother was awake and sitting at the kitchen table. "I've made up the spare room," she said.

Then I suppose I floored all three of them. "She's staying with me," I said. In my room, of course, but I didn't have to say it.

Gloria looked shocked. My parents' jaws dropped the way you see them do it in movies. Their sixteen-year-old son had just told them he was going to be sleeping with a girl in his room. Yet no one said a word as I led Gloria by the hand upstairs to my bedroom, closed the door, and locked it.

When the door was closed, Gloria said my name out loud. The formal one. "Joseph?" I don't know what the question part was because she didn't say any more than that, but it was one hell of a question. And then she kissed me. I tasted the salt on her lips from where the tears had fallen.

Here's the thing. I had a flashback of how alone I'd felt after the news of my parents' death. I don't think I had ever or will ever feel so alone again. I was horribly afraid. My vision of a future—any future—had disappeared. I felt totally abandoned. I imagined myself sliding down a steep slope to a dark, dark place. I desperately wanted someone who cared for me to help me and not ever leave me alone again. But that someone had not been there. Now I was Gloria's someone.

"I'll sleep on a blanket on the floor," I said. "You take my bed."

She nodded, sat on the edge of my bed, took off her shoes, and let one fall to the floor. We both jumped. And then gave each other a look.

"Sorry about your parents," I said.

She shrugged. Then she got into bed with her clothes on and watched me.

I tossed a blanket on the floor, found a spare pillow and another blanket in the closet, and lay down there. It was much harder than I'd expected. And I'd forgotten to turn out the light. When I got up again to do so, Gloria said, "I need you to hold me."

I turned the switch off and we were in darkness. Then I walked to the bed and got in with her. We were both fully clothed. I put my arm around her and held her.

And we both fell asleep.

◄ ■ ►

We rather fouled up the use of language by referring to sex as "sleeping" with someone. Sleeping together, fully clothed, or not, is an amazing thing. Guess what? I had never slept with someone before. No one. The circumstances were not great but the sleeping together was wonderful. I liked her warmth. I liked breathing her breath. I liked the fact that we could kiss. I liked her body next to mine and, yes, I did get somewhat aroused.

But this was not about sex.

This was about caring.

There was a phone call in the middle of the night. One of my parents must have fielded that one. No one woke us up.

You might think that when we woke up the next morning, we might have been surprised to discover we were in bed together. But we weren't. We were very cool. Gloria was leaning on an elbow looking at me when I first opened my eyes. She was smiling. I had never seen her smile that way. Ever.

"Thank you," she said.

I just smiled back at her.

So we got up, rumpled clothes and all. We went downstairs. My dad had left for the store but my mom was there. She made breakfast for us and talked about the weather. There were no questions about last night. "Do you want me to drive you to school?" she asked. "I phoned my office and said I'd be in late."

I looked at Gloria. She shook her head no.

"We're taking the day off," I said. "What do you call it? A mental health day?"

My mom smiled. "Gloria, I talked to your mother. She was upset you left but she knows you're okay."

Gloria nodded.

And then we ate breakfast. And Gloria washed the dishes. And my mom left for work. And we were alone.

"Now what?" Gloria asked.

"Now I take you to one of my favorite places on the planet," I said.

"Can I brush my teeth first?"

"Sure."

"Can I use your toothbrush?"

"Absolutely."

◄ ■ ►

I report all this to you, realizing how sentimental and goofy romantic it must sound. I remind you that I am not a knight in shining armor and that it may actually be you, Gloria, who one day hears all this. But if it is you, it will be many years in the future. And I don't know how our lives will have turned out. Or it could be some stranger who listens to this decades down the line and finds it a bizarre and curious artifact of a human life. In fact, I've dipped back into this diary and noticed many inconsistencies in what I report.

I say that nothing makes sense, yet I sometimes act as if things have deep meaning. I know. But you will have to accept my story for what it is. *My story*. Life still does not make a whole lot of sense. Gloria's mother and father should be perfectly happy. Nobody cheated on anybody. They have health, income, a beautiful, smart daughter. But something has made it impossible for them to be happy.

As you might guess, I took Gloria to the forest. We skipped school and went to the woods. We didn't talk that much. I pointed to things—oak trees, blue jays, moss. I was able to make Gloria's sadness go away. For a while.

But later in the day it came back.

"I feel that it's all my fault. My parents are breaking up because of something I did or didn't do."

"I doubt that is the case."

"And now I've drawn you into this. Now I've made you suffer."

That didn't make sense. "How have I suffered?"

She really didn't have an answer. "You missed school."

"I call that real torture," I said.

"But I've got you entangled."

"I like that word. Entangled. I like the feeling of being entangled."

Later that day, I walked her home, and her mother was there, and they both hugged and cried, and I went in and had an awkward snack in the kitchen.

I felt great about the night together, the day together, the whole wonderful entanglement of it all. But here's the kicker.

When I left Gloria, I felt sad again immediately. On the walk home, I felt more alone than ever. I would sit in my room and watch a movie. Alone. And then go to bed. Alone.

I felt more abandoned than ever. I could reflect on how good it had been to be with Gloria. How totally NOT alone it all was. How we had come together and shared sadness and then, dare I say, happiness. And then it ended. And I wasn't convinced we'd ever be able to revisit that island of a night and day that was so entirely shared.

As I drifted off to sleep, I slipped again down that slope into darkness. In my dream, the police were knocking at the door again. But in my dream I believed that all I had to do was *not* open the door and my parents would still be alive. And my life would go on as normal.

The only mistake I had made was opening that damn door.

CHAPTER TWELVE

JOSEPH STALIN—NASTY GUY. JOE DIMAGGIO—BASEBALL PLAYER who married Marilyn Monroe. Joseph Conrad—author who wrote *Heart of Darkness*, which we had to read in English. Very dark. Joseph Smith—had to look him up. Founder of the Mormons who come around here in white shirts and ties on a Saturday morning. Thought it was okay for a man to have more than one wife. Joseph—father of Christ. Well, he doesn't even get credit as a biological father. Christ was sort of adopted, you might say, or he was the result of a kind of early artificial insemination project on God's part.

God. At some point I should discuss God, although I am not and probably never will be an expert on this subject. Right now I'm just at work on my name. All the Joes I can think of. This to stave off chaos and confusion. Gloria is not returning my phone calls. She's not answering her cell.

Dean has called me twice and left messages. "Dude, I think I figured something out. Call me."

"Joe, I'm a little confused on this so if you could call me, I'd like you to hear what I have to say." No, I can't do Dean-world right now. This is the world according to Joe. I'm doing this to occupy my mind. To connect the dots of all the Joes. We are all related, I profess. Even me and Jesus' father.

Not God. The other one. Joseph of Nazareth.

Other Joes I can think of. There are Saint Josephs—more than one. We are that holy. But I'll have to look them up. Maybe I'll turn out to be another one but I don't think so. Oh, another Biblical one—Joseph from the Old Testament who had been given a coat of many colors by his father. Then there's Joseph Kennedy, JFK's father who, I think, made all his money in illegal booze. Do I have that right? Joe Louis was a boxer. Joe McCarthy was a senator who ruined hundreds of Americans' lives by calling them Communists in the 1950s. He and Stalin were in the Bad Joe camp, for sure. I bet there were others. All us Joes can't be saints, you know.

And then there is me. Joseph Campbell. Not exactly famous, I know. A young school teacher named Celia Wright meets a metal band lead guitarist. Turns out his name is Henry Campbell. She gets pregnant. I am born. They debate, so the story goes, about two hundred somewhat exotic names. Give up and call me something ordinary. Joseph. Joseph Campbell. One of my earliest recollections of school is someone calling me Campbell Soup as soon as the teacher said my name. And it stuck, of course. That and the fact that I drank too much Pepsi one day and accidentally peed my pants. I vividly remember that day in grade one. Brian Deveau raising his hand to tell Ms. Schwartz, "Hey, Ms. Schwartz, Campbell Soup just peed his pants."

It takes a while to recover from such humiliation. I never drank Pepsi again, nor did I urinate during class time. One lesson learned in life.

And this reminds me of something. Get this. My little lack of bladder control was the worst thing that ever happened to me in life up to that point. No kidding. My life had been so non-traumatic that this seemed like the end of the world as we know it. More than that. It *remained* the "worst day of my life" right up until ... well ... you know.

Up until twelve, I had been, as they say, an Ordinary Joe. And so I should have remained. I went searching on the Net for other Joe words. The Joes were once considered the blues in the 1950s. As in depression. As in, "Gloria has the Joes."

There was once a guy named Joe College. He dressed and acted the part of someone going to university. Not a bad term, really, but there it is.

Joe Schmo was another one. "Yeah, who says? Joe Schmo?" This from an old, old movie I saw once. Joe Schmo never appeared on screen. He, too, was average and not all that bright. Joe Blow seems to be about the same. That'd be a tough one to be named as a kid and my guess is that if there ever was a Blow family, they changed their last name.

I think there must have been Joe Crow somewhere and he could have hung out with Joe Blow and Joe Schmo but probably not with Surfer Joe, who appeared on the scene in the early 1960s and was—you guessed it—an average surfer.

So my name is associated with all of these things. From helping to raise a savior—to representing all that is average in a male. So how, I might ask, can I go back to being an Ordinary Joe?

The answer is that I cannot do this. I am the sum total of my parts. I was assembled, prepared to meet the world (very nicely, thank you), then later shredded and glued back together and set adrift.

◄ ■ ►

My dad comes home and knocks on my door. He looks tired.

"Come in," I say.

"Everything okay?" The generic all-purpose question.

"I'm still worried about Gloria."

"It's pretty tough when parents go through hard times."

"Any advice?"

"Be a good friend."

"I think we may be more than that now," I say. I had decided I could talk to my dad. I was pretty sure he would understand.

"Oh," he says, jumping to conclusions. A pregnant pause. "You guys, didn't ... um ... do anything the other night?" He looks a little embarrassed.

"There was nothing sexual about it." And this, as noted, was not one hundred percent true, but we didn't really do anything. And clothes were on, remember?

"Well, if you ever need to talk ..." His voice trails off, suggesting that he hopes like hell we never have to talk about it but he'd give it a shot if he had to. Neither of my parents has ever had the sex talk with me. Hell, I don't think ninety-nine percent of parents do that anymore. There's just so much stuff out there, so, like, what could they say?

"Thanks, Dad. Do you know much about depression?"

"A bit. Gloria, right?"

"Well, yeah. But I think I've been there."

"Of course. When you were first with us. The doctors said we had to watch you."

"What did you do?"

"We watched you."

"And?"

"And you got better."

"Not totally," I say.

"I think I know that. Still have bad days?"

"Yeah. But I'm coping."

"I know you are. But Gloria—you're worried, right?"

"She's been down for a while. I thought I was helping, but I'm not sure it's enough."

"Tell her to try some evening primrose oil, some melatonin maybe, and some 5-HTP. I'll bring some home."

"And that will help?"

"It might help but it won't cure. Her heart is breaking because her parents are breaking up. I've seen it too many times. Parents fight, kids get damaged."

"You and mom never fight."

"We do it quietly and away from you. But nothing major."

"Thanks."

"You're welcome. Call Gloria."

And he leaves. I suppose some kids have fathers that come home drunk or make impossible rules for their kids or scream and yell when the lawn mower doesn't work. But not Will. Will eats a lot of vegetables and a handful of organic supplements. He has a calm, quiet way about him and I liked him as a person ever since he first came into my life. Sometimes I wished he was more interesting, more exciting, even a little crazier, like Henry was when he was young. But most of the time I'm cool with who Will is. He seems to understand how the world works—the good and the bad of it—and he's okay with that. He doesn't have plans to become wealthy or famous or change the world. But he tries to be helpful to his customers with advice about selenium, evening primrose, and such.

My dad's idea of doing something totally crazy is sitting outside in the backyard on a summer afternoon and letting himself get a sunburn while drinking three beers and eating a bag of salted pretzels. Wild and crazy or what?

◄ ■ ►

Still no answer from Gloria. It's getting late in the evening. I'm hoping she is just sleeping.

Dean is calling again.

"Joe, it's Dean." As if I wouldn't recognize his voice. "Joe, I've been thinking." This is often a bad sign. "All that stuff people post about me."

"It's crap. None of it is true. You shouldn't pay any attention to it."

"I know. Most of it is not true. But it hurts."

"So don't read it. Turn your computer off. Read some books about marine biology. Study sharks."

"I will. I promise. But Oliver posted something about me."

"Oliver is a class-A turd."

"I know. But he said that I'm a faggot."

"He called me a homo for saying hi to him once in the hallway. So he thinks you're gay. Ignore it."

"No. I think he may be right."

"You think. You're not sure?"

"I'm not sure about much. But I *am* different."

"That doesn't necessarily make you gay."

"But I've considered the possibility."

"Do you really like guys?"

"Some."

"Do you like girls?"

"Some."

"I'm not convinced."

"But what should I do?"

"I don't know. What if you are gay?"

"That's what I was thinking. What if I am? Would you still be my friend?"

I didn't know what to say at first. This was beyond weird and I was a little freaked. "If I saw you staring at me in the washroom, I might get worried. But I've known you a long time, dude. I don't think you're gay."

"But I'm still not sure. Maybe I just haven't met the right girl."

"Probably not."

"But you'd be okay with it if I was?"

I was still kind of freaked, but I didn't want to say what I really felt. Instead I laughed. "Totally. They say straight guys should have at least one gay friend to advise them on things like what clothes to wear and what women really want. I read that in a magazine."

"But I'm not sure I'm gay. So don't tell anyone."

"I won't."

"I feel better."

"Good."

I'm back to thinking about my old plan to strategically place dog crap in the path of Oliver's feet. I think it may be worth the effort. I realize it may turn out that Dean, who has been a friend of mine forever, might actually be gay. But he's pretty unsure of—well, just about everything. So I'll give it time. If he is gay, he's going to have to build some confidence about it. It's hard enough being sixteen and straight. Gays must have one hell of a set of challenges. As for me, I'm pretty sure I'm just an Ordinary Joe. Straight. Damaged. And trying to find the silver thread that ties everything together.

Not that I ever expect to find it. The world is way too screwed up for that. It's just that part of me keeps searching, despite the fact that it is hopeless.

CHAPTER THIRTEEN

IT'S BEEN OVER A WEEK SINCE MY LAST ENTRY. WHAT HAPPENED? YOU might wonder. Well, go back and listen to the last part of that last entry.

I hit a wall. I decided the digital diary thing was messing up my head. I replayed some of what I'd recorded later that same night and found it puzzling. Maybe some things should just *be*, I decided. Recording and analyzing everything like that did not make me feel any better. It did not help me understand things better. Who was I to be able to help anyone? Dean? Gloria?

But as you can see, I'm back. My dad asked me how the DD was going. I told him I quit. He said he was fine with that. Typical for my dad. Never pushy. Very organic in his approach to business, life, and raising a son.

So, of course, here I am. Hello. I'm back. Is it for him? For Gloria (who I still think may listen to this someday)? Or is it for me? I really don't know. But I am back after my ... what's the word? ... hiatus. From the Latin, I think. A break in continuity. A gap. A missing link in a chain of events. Or get this ... a new word for you, I bet. A lacuna.

A breather. A rest. A pause. It seems logical to think that as I move through my life, my sequence of random events, there is a place where a gap occurs. But I would be lying if I said that nothing happened during this past week. A lot did happen during Joe's lacunic absence from his digital diary.

First, I guess you could say that depression is infectious. Coming back down from my exultant first co-sleeping event with a member of the opposite sex, as you may have noted, I fell into that pit. That basement of despair. That dark place. Gloria's own unhappiness had opened up a wound. And then she went away.

Gloria and her mother went to stay with Gloria's grandmother, a three-hour drive from here. She would not let me know the phone number there and she did not answer my calls to her cell phone. Instead, I received short text messages like this: "Am ok. At G'mom's till things chill. Be kind." Or cryptic e-mails like this: "Went to Grandmom's doc and he prescribed some meds. Mother and daughter on pharmaceuticals. All is well. Can sleep now. Thanks for helping me. Love. G."

At first I had this terrifying fear that it was just a first step. Maybe soon Gloria and her mom would be gone, possibly for good. Isn't this what happens sometimes when a family breaks up? A good chance I'd never see her again. Never hold her in my arms like that night. And why didn't she at least take my phone call or call me?

I drifted through my dark days, my only real diversion being Dean and his current situation. Most of school was just a fog—kind of like the way it had been for me right after the accident. But this was a bit different. As I drifted from one class to the next, I found myself thinking dark thoughts. What if Gloria was a blip? A one-of-a-kind thing in my life. A good thing. A good thing gone. And I had failed somehow to really help her.

But let's leave that there for the time being, because I don't know what more to say about it. One more shift. Random can be good. Random can be bad.

◀ ■ ▶

As you can see, I had to break that one off. This is later the same night. I tried to sleep but couldn't, so, as usual, anything goes here. Skip over this part if you want. And remember, there is no story line here. No deeper meaning. Just a boy and his microphone headset, staring out at a dark night.

So let's talk about education to get one's mind off personal things.

Eighty-seven percent of what you learn in school is of little value, let us assume. Some would argue that percentage is higher, some lower. But let's not be cynical for a minute and realize that eighty-seven percent leaves a full thirteen percent as something useful. Let's call it knowledge. My school, in its infinite wisdom (just joking), had just this year come up with elective mini-courses on various unlikely topics. You could choose one class that met for only one period a week on subjects like this: surreal art, experimental music, contemporary poetry, astronomy, the history of magic, eastern religions, or ancient Greek philosophy.

There were only eight of us who chose ancient Greek philosophy, which must have sounded like a real yawner compared to the history of magic. The course is taught by Dr. Henson Langley. Langley was in his last year before retirement. He was completely bald, but had a goatee for a beard.

His eyes were fierce and he scared a lot of kids, which is how he had survived a long career as a mathematics teacher. All he had to do was look straight at you and it was like a laser beam burning a hole.

But I liked him. He was for real. "It's my last year," he told us first day of class. "I've endured plenty. I've taken my share of crap from students and administration alike. I don't think they can fire me, so this year I feel that I should speak my mind freely. What is discussed in this classroom is to stay in this classroom. Whatever I say, whatever you say. There will be no tests, no final exam, no papers. You will be graded on your attendance and your questions. That's probably the way we should have been running schools for these past several centuries but we screwed it up somehow."

He was serious. All you had to do was show up and ask questions.

Well, as previously noted, I was wandering the hallways Gloria-less and fell into my seat in Langley's class somewhat somnambulant. Aristotle had been invoked before but today was something new. Langley told us about one of big A's big theories. And I perked up a little and noted in my mind's memory stick a lecture that went something like this:

"Aristotle, as you remember, lived 384 to 322 BC. If you lived BC the years went down each time a new year came around, but, of course, they didn't see it that way. Aristotle suggested that in order to understand anything, you could ask four questions. It's call the Theory of Causes but the word 'cause' is misleading. But then many things in life can be misleading. I'm sure you've noted that in your mere fifteen or sixteen years of human existence. So, let's suppose you come across, I don't know, let's say a non-human sentient being during lunch in the cafeteria. Aristotle would suggest you not be startled but instead try to answer the following. One: *what is it made of?* If the answer is mozzarella cheese, you have a start at understanding. But let's move on. Question two: *what is its form or essence?* It appears to have a head, eyes, arms, legs, and is speaking a language that is not English. Three: *what produced it?* Does it have a mother and a father or was it created by a demented genius cheese maker? Four, and here's the really tough one: *what is its purpose?* This, Aristotle and others refer to as 'final cause.' What is the reason for this sentient being's existence?"

We were all, I suppose, a bit bug-eyed, if for no other reason, by the way that Langley had become animated, excited to a point that little bits of frothing white spit appeared on the corners of his mouth. "Now, if we apply Aristotle's fourth question to our own existence, what do we come up with?"

A very special kind of silence filled the room. Cynic that I am, you can understand that it takes a lot to impress me. I was having a bad week, all existence filtered by the sadness and confusion of Gloria's running away with her mother. But it occurred to me that the very silence that filled the room just then was the pure unadulterated sound of real education. We were in the thirteen percent territory. And this subject matter was edging onto my own turf here. So I blurted it out. "The fourth question can't be answered. We can never truly know what our purpose is."

Those fierce eyes were upon me now. I had broken the silence. "Why would you say that, Joseph?"

I held his gaze for once. "Because we are human. We search for meaning; we settle for easy answers so we won't go crazy; and then we get lazy. We ignore the obvious truth."

"Which is?"

"There is no meaning. No purpose."

A few more seconds of good educational silence. I expected to be crucified. After all, wasn't I suggesting Aristotle's theory was futile? But Langley let me off the hook. "Anyone else care to dive in here?"

There were no divers. So Langley moved on to other Aristotelian notions. When class was over, he called me to his desk before I could sneak out of the room. "Do you really believe what you said?" he asked, his demeanor much softer now.

"Yes," I said, "I think I do."

"I know it's fashionable to say such things when you are young but you seem so confident in the way you said it. Why?"

"Did you ever lose anyone very close to you?" I heard myself say, shocked that I had leaped to this.

Totally out of character, Dr. Langley dropped his eyes to the floor. "A son," he said. "A long time ago."

"Did you ever lose two people that were very close to you—both at the same time?" I heard myself ask and I don't know why I said what I said just then.

He looked up. "No," he said.

Students for the next class were now coming into the room. "I'm sorry," Langley said, now sounding nothing like a teacher. And I'd heard a lot of sorrys in my time but his was one of the most sincere. It was too bad the school was going to lose this guy after this year. Thirteen percent was about to drop a bit lower.

◀ ■ ▶

Of course, the rumors of Dean's gayness (not by him but by gossipers and creeps on the Internet) had spread and I had to decide if I could handle being seen with him, walking the halls or going into the lavatories to take a pee or sitting with him in the cafeteria. A lot of people thought I was weird enough already, and if they decided I was both weird and gay, I, too, would suffer the slings and arrows. I admit I avoided him once when I saw him in the hallway. Then twice.

Then I was angry at myself and—maybe it was loneliness without Gloria around or something more noble—I met up with him at his locker one day not long after the Aristotle session.

"Deaner," I said. "Where ya been all week?" As if I wasn't the one avoiding him.

"Joe. Good to see you, man."

Two girls walking by just then winked at me in a funny way. Oh, great.

"We gotta talk," I said.

"Yeah, that'd be great. I've been doing some research."

That was just like Dean. Not all that great at school, a monumentally poor speller, a total-panicked white-knuckled test-taker, a kid who lost his ability to speak when called on in class. But if he got something new in his head—whether it was life on Mars, the Mariana Trench, or homosexuality—he'd read some books and look stuff up on the Internet.

It was the end of the school day. I should have been out front waiting for my bus, but the truth was I didn't want to go home and be by myself. Dean had been my friend through thick and thin. In fact, he had been my first friend when I moved here and started school. True, he had grown a little stranger over the years I'd known him. I don't mean the gay thing. Just the way he withdrew sometimes and the way he acted.

"Let's go get some coffee," I said.

"Really?"

"Really," I said. It was true; everyone would see us walking away from school. It would all be reported on someone's idiot blog site. Someone would see us at the Second Cup as well. I, too, would be a target for the local cyber bullies and I didn't look forward to that, but then, Dean was Dean, whatever sexual persuasion he was.

Dean wanted a cappuccino and I ordered a black coffee. I picked the table by the window for us to sit at. I was feeling defiant. As if on cue, a couple of guys from school—Tim and Devon—the two most obviously gay guys from our class, walked in and past our table. Devon just nodded but Tim gave us both a broad smile. A couple of Rachelle's girlfriends were at a table near the back and had already had us in their sights. I figured that this pretty well sealed the deal.

"I read that it's at least ten percent of the population," Dean said. "Probably more."

"Then it's no big deal," I said.

"Yeah, but it is. If I'm gay, it changes the way I see myself. It changes the way people see me. I'm pretty confused."

"What exactly makes you think you are gay?" I asked.

"I like looking at guys. Not all guys. Just some guys."

"Like who?"

"Well, like you, for example."

"Oh, shit."

"Sorry," Dean replied, now looking a little embarrassed.

"Well, do you like looking at girls?"

"Some of them, too."

"Ever make out with a guy?" I asked.

"No. But I never made out with a girl, either."

"I'd say you're ambivalent."

"Oh, no. What does that mean?"

"It just means you're uncertain," I explained. "Maybe you are gay. Maybe straight. Maybe bisexual."

"I've thought about that, too. But it seems pretty complicated. I'm confused. I'd like to know for sure."

"Maybe it doesn't work that way," I tried to assure him.

He nodded toward Tim and Devon, who were trying not to stare at us. "Some people seem confident."

"But that's not your style. I think confusion is okay. Uncertainty is okay. I'd give it all some time before starting to change your wardrobe."

"What do you mean?"

"It was sort of a joke. I mean, just take your time."

"So if I decide that I'm sure that I'm gay, would you still be my friend?"

"Hell, yes," I said. "Just relax and give it some time. You still thinking of being a marine biologist, or does this change things?"

"No, I'm still thinking that's the way to go. I'd like being out on the ocean."

I got some of those looks the next day in school. At first it bothered me and then, after a while, I got used to it. I started giving eye contact to the girls who stared and they just smiled, most of them. But when I did it to a couple of the guys, they looked right away. It was funny how it made me feel. It was like I had some kind of power over them, and that made me feel just a little more at home in the world than the day before.

CHAPTER FOURTEEN

SUPPOSE SOMEONE IS LISTENING TO THIS ONE HUNDRED YEARS FROM now. Suppose this is all that is left of the world I grew up in. Imagine trying to mine each entry for information about the early twenty-first century from my life, my thoughts, my lunatic ravings. If I could step outside of myself and listen to my entries from the beginning, it's possible I would begin to detect a pattern. To my thoughts. To my tangents. To my ramblings and ravings. But, as you can see for yourself, there are many loose threads, many unanswered questions. In a random universe where lives like mine are ruled by random gods of chance and change, you keep your eyes open and watch for the next stone thrown at you.

The random universe giveth and taketh away, to use a Biblical phrase.

Gloria returned to me today. But she was an altered Gloria. And, at first, I feared I had lost her for good ... if I had ever had her at all.

Our night of sleeping together seemed to both of us like something that had happened a hundred years ago. Her eyes were kind of dull and her skin looked pale. She walked rather slowly and she slouched. She didn't seem all that excited to see me when I caught up with her in the school hallway.

"How was your week with your mother?" I asked.

"I survived it."

"Survival is good."

"Not always," she said.

"Gloria?"

"What?"

"What happened?"

The sigh. The great, hopeless human sigh. She stared at the wall.

"Please," I said.

Another sigh. She turned towards me. "My mom already has a lawyer."

"Divorce sucks," I said. I had a flash of my own first parents for some reason. And I felt that twinge of anger at their loss. All those other parents out there. All they had to do was work it out, not throw it away. The silly bastards. All they needed to do was work out the details. Not toss it away, not ruin a son or daughter.

"She wants us to move."

"No way," I said, feeling anger rise.

"I told her I wouldn't move. I said I'd stay here and live with my father."

"Is that want you want?"

"No. I said it to hurt her. I want to live with my father *and* my mother. She said that will never happen again."

"You're sixteen. You should get to decide where you live."

"What if I have to live back and forth—one week here, one week there? Wherever *there* is."

"You shouldn't have to do that."

"My mom made me go to the doctor. She said I should go

on medication."

"Antidepressant?"

"Yes."

"Does it make you feel stoned?"

"No. It makes me feel a little numb. Emotionally, that is."

"Is it better?"

"I'm still depressed. I just don't seem to care as much."

"Kind of takes the edge off, takes some of the hurt away?"

"It kind of takes everything away."

"Not good."

She shook her head. "No. Not good."

"Stop taking it."

"I don't know. I may need it to get through this."

"Come sleep with me again," I blurted rather loudly so that a couple of our classmates heard.

At least that took her out of the fog. "Shh," Gloria shushed me. "I can't do that. Not now, anyway. I have to try to stay with my mom and help her through this. And I have to spend some time with my dad, who is living in an apartment over top of his friend's garage. I have to try to let him know I still care about him, too."

"But I want you to fall asleep with me again sometime. I want to hold you in my arms."

She smiled now. "I loved that part."

"I promise I'll be good," I heard myself say. Which I guess meant that I was offering up some code of good behavior. I wouldn't try to turn sleeping into sex. Maybe someday but not now.

"That's sweet," she said.

"Gloria," I said. "I'll help you get through this."

"I know you will." And I thought she was going to kiss me on the cheek or something but instead she just hugged me. It was a good hug. She held on for what seemed like some very long seconds.

There have been a few phone calls from Dean. He's still confused. Identity issues. Not sure one way or the other. He hasn't discussed it with his parents. "Why let them in on my confusion?" he says. He's started working on a list of famous gay people. He even claims Aristotle was gay. How would anyone know this? And the list continues. "James Dean. Melissa Etheridge. Elton John. Edward II of England. Peter the Great, who was a Russian czar. Rock Hudson. J. Edgar Hoover."

I call it the Dean's List. He's enlightening me about famous gay people. Maybe this information will be useful to me someday if I end up on a TV game show. I decided to look some of these people up. Rock Hudson. J. Edgar Hoover. They were alive at the same time and, of course, this was before gay marriage was acceptable. But what if Rock Hudson, the suave, sophisticated Hollywood actor, had married J. Edgar Hoover, the brutish head of the FBI?

◀ ■ ▶

I can't help but compare my own state of affairs to both Dean's and Gloria's. I am fairly secure in my sexual identity and can only begin to imagine how confused Dean must be. I mean, Dean has always been confused about almost everything, but this one must really have him befuddled. And Gloria, trying to adjust to the breakup of her parents. And then there is me. What about me?

Not gay. Dependable parents. Feeling a little stronger. But

there is this thing ahead of me I have to do. Some illusory quest. I know only vaguely what it is.

I open my closet and take out the Stratocaster. It's way out of tune. I do a rough job of tuning it. I haul out the mini-amp that's been in there gathering dust. I never really learned to play guitar very well. I know a handful of chords. I plug in the amp. I find a guitar pick. Plug in the Strat. I hit an A-minor chord and then a G. I hit them over and over. When I look up, I realize the photo of Henry and Seal on my dresser has been lying face down. For how long, I don't know. I set the picture back upright and look at the smiles on those faces. I look for me in their faces. I see my nose, my lips. Dad's hair. Mom's eyes. I keep hitting the two chords over and over. I don't think I did a very good job tuning the guitar. And I'm back there all of a sudden. The living room of my old house in Riverside. There is a fire in the fireplace. My dad is practicing on the guitar. He's talking about starting another band. A "garage band," he calls it. A weekend band. My mom looks up from the book she is reading and says she thinks it's a great idea. Dad starts to make up some words for a song he is attempting to write. He was not a very good songwriter and never a great singer. He wrote down endless fragments of songs he got in his head, most of which he never finished. I have this feeling they are in a box somewhere.

I keep hitting those two chords over and over and feel a surge of something powerful welling up within me. I can't label this feeling. I really can't. All I know is that it scares the hell out of me. So I stop playing. Unplug the amp. Put the Strat back into the case.

◄ ■ ►

For the hell of it, I Google my name on the Internet. There is, of course, nothing posted about me. I am a nobody. But nonetheless "Joseph Campbell" brings some interesting results. Joseph and his brother founded the Campbell Soup Company in Camden, New Jersey, in 1897. Not long before they went into the business and turned the Delaware River red with leftover tomato pulp, most people thought tomatoes were poisonous. It's a funny world, this one we live in.

But then there is the other Joseph Campbell. Born March 26, 1904, in White Plains, New York. Died October 30, 1987. An author. Had something to do with mythology and world religions. There is a quote there by him. "Mythology is often referred to as other people's religions, and religion can be defined as misinterpreted mythology." What the hell does that mean? I try to make some sense of the write-up here. It seems that Mr. Campbell pissed some people off by writing that *all* religions are concerned with the search for the ultimate source from which everything comes. And here's the kicker. That source is "unknowable" because it existed before words or knowledge. Oh, boy, I think. These are large ideas. But the "unknowable" part starts to make some crazy kind of sense to me. I swallow hard. There is something else here. My eyes go blurry.

There is a list of books the man wrote, this other Joe Campbell, the one who did not produce tomato soup. The titles sound academic and totally unfamiliar. All except for one. I feel something akin to an electric shock race down my spine. I see my father sitting on the floor of the living room with handwritten pages scattered around him. Those fragments of lyrics for songs that will never be finished.

And I see my mother again, sitting in a chair by a lamp. She is reading a book.

I stand up and realize I am sweating. I can feel it dripping down from my armpits. I leave my room and go down two flights. The house is empty. I'm home alone. I open up a closet in the basement. A place I've been avoiding for years. I turn on an overhead light with the string hanging down. The unlabeled boxes are stacked neatly. There is dust. I know which box I am looking for. It is different from the rest. It once held a television set. The TV that once sat in my old living room. The TV is long gone but the box is still here. It's heavier than I expect as I pick it up, set it down on the floor, and open it. More dust.

Opening the lid of that box takes me an almost superhuman effort. I continue to sweat, even though it is not very warm here. My eyes still have a hard time focusing. But I am looking at old manila folders with Henry's song lyrics. I recognize his handwriting. I lift them gently and set them down on the floor. Beneath them are old books. Poetry. Novels. A couple of old textbooks from university—psychology, education, history. And then this. *The Hero with a Thousand Faces*. By Joseph Campbell. I lift it ever so slowly out of the box and run my hand over the cover.

I open the book and, on the first blank page, I see my father's handwriting:

For Celia, with all my love,
Henry

CHAPTER FIFTEEN

ANOTHER DAY ON PLANET EARTH. AND NOW I KNOW THAT I AM either the namesake of one of the founders of Campbell Soup or a man who believed all religions were fundamentally the same. I have to assume the latter. I don't think I ever heard my mother actually come out and say I was named this way. But it must be true. I am holding that book right now. I am smelling the dusty smell of it. In its introduction, the author quotes someone with the unlikely name of Rig Vedic. "Ekam Sat Vipra Bahuda Vadanthi." Fortunately, there is a translation: "Truth is one. The sages speak of it by many names." Do you see what I'm up against here?

What do you suppose my parents expected of me? Was I to be a seeker of truth? A unifier of religions? A hero with a thousand faces? It's all a bit too much.

Instead, I am a boy. A confused boy. In search of what?

I smell the book again and I am taken back to a quiet evening. I am alone with my mother this time. And she is reading. Perhaps this was the book she was reading. Perhaps something else. I am trying to remember why my father is not there that night and I remember that, for a while, he had a part-time job in the evenings working at a 7-Eleven. They needed the extra money to help pay the mortgage.

So there were quiet evenings like this. Seal and me. She read books. I read comic books. I had boxes of them. But they are all gone. I did not bring them with me. After the accident, I never read a comic book again. And I never went to one single movie based on any superhero. In fact, I've only gone to a very few movie theaters in my life. And on those times when I did, I felt nauseous and sometimes had to leave early.

I started reading Joseph Campbell but then I set him aside. It was tough sledding. Suffice it to say, he seemed to have dedicated his life to finding patterns, similarities in world religions, themes. Meaning. Clearly, he was still highly thought of, long after his death, October 30, 1987, at the age of 83 in Honolulu. He must have liked warm weather and palm trees. From his photo on the back of the book—still a young man here—he looked remarkably average. Like somebody's father who is manager of a doughnut shop. That's what he looked like to me.

During spring break, I worked at my father's store the whole week, helping out with inventory. The kava kava was running low. Echinacea was as popular as ever. Customers ask a lot of questions of you while you are doing inventory. My father encouraged me to take long breaks and study some of the books he had about vitamins, herbs, and nutrition. I learned that kava kava is derived from an herbal drink—actually an alcoholic drink that Tahitians use to get very stoned and have visions. I wonder if J.C. ever partook of such rituals. He most certainly must have had a few of his own vision quests.

I also read about milk thistle. An old English herbalist said it was, "the best remedy that grows against all melancholy diseases." The silymarin in the thistle heals the liver and is chock full of antioxidants. And in most parts of the world, the thistle is considered a nasty, prickly weed—except in Scotland where it is the national flower. I read about quinine and coltsfoot and comfrey and coconut oil and coenzyme Q-10 and glucosamine and beta-carotene and garlic. God. You'd think you could save the world if you could only get everyone to eat enough garlic.

It wasn't until a slow Wednesday afternoon that the most obvious thing popped into my head. *It all came from plants.* Maybe some of it worked, maybe some of it didn't. But it *all* came from plants. The pills and the capsules and the soft gels and all the liquids and tinctures—the stuff that worked in them all—were derived from some plant that grew out of the ground. And if you studied long and hard enough, rooting around into the chemical makeup of the plant and the chemical makeup of a human being, there was an explanation as to why Echinacea helped prevent you from getting a cold or the flu, why kava kava calmed you down, why glucosamine helped your aching joints, and why horny goat weed made you horny as a goat.

From bilberry to cohosh to ginseng and green tea extract, from aloe vera to wild yam root and yohimbe—they all came from plants and they all had the potential to improve your health. It was in that quiet time on that Wednesday that the pieces of this one puzzle started to fit together, causing a most blasphemous idea to take root in my brain. *It was as if there was some grand design.* It was as if everything we needed—for sustenance and health, at least—was right here already, growing somewhere on the planet. Quite possibly, right beneath our feet in the form of what today we'd call a weed—chamomile, chickweed, dock, dandelion, angelica. Need I go on?

I realized that on more than one occasion, Will had tried to get me interested in all this. His lectures had fallen on deaf ears. But it was my week off from school. Did you ever realize that on a week off from school, you actually end up learning much more than a week when you are in school? Is this not ironic?

So for much of the week, I stocked shelves, I took many breaks, and I read. As long as I had a book or a magazine in my hands, my father did not say a word. Imagine how strange it must have seemed to him—me sitting quietly in the uphol-stered chair in the corner in the back where customers were allowed to read from his small library of health books, right there by the amino acids, the rose hip extracts, the barley grass supplements, and the pumpkin seed oil. Me. Reading.

There was this one time when I heard the little bell ring as a customer entered the store. It had annoyed me early on in the week but now I barely noticed it. I was thinking that I should go back to my inventory work or maybe help my father with the cash register. I'd do that from time to time to give him a break. But sometimes I screwed up and had to go get him to set things right.

When I stood up, I was shocked but more than a little thrilled to see Gloria. But she wasn't alone. Dean was with her. That was totally weird.

"I thought you had gone away to your grandmother's again," I said to Gloria. She'd been incommunicado again for days and I'd given up trying to get in touch.

"I was starting to hate it. My mom does nothing but bad-mouth my father. So I came back. I'm staying with my dad. But it's not much better."

"Dean, good to see you, too, dude." I said. Truth was I'd been trying to avoid Dean. I hadn't returned his phone calls, was getting a little weary of his identity dilemma.

"Nice outfit," was all he said. He was referring to the rather official-looking green smock I wore. Dad said I didn't have to wear it if I didn't want to but he wore one. It did add an air of professionalism, even to a sixteen-year-old, and the customers seemed to treat you with more respect—like a doctor, I suppose. Or a health food guru. Or a shaman.

I was still a little confused. Dean and Gloria together. Tracking me down here at work. "What's up?" I asked.

"We were worried about you," Dean said.

I looked at Gloria. She nodded. My jaw dropped. I wanted to say, *You were worried about me?* out loud, but I stifled it.

Gloria looked more like Gloria, I realized. The old Gloria. Maybe the meds had kicked in. Or maybe she'd stopped taking them. Their visit had been her idea. Dean was the side-kick. Dean would always be the sidekick. "I told Dean about Charlene," she said.

"The bitch," Dean said.

"But I'm okay. I'm over that."

"But you went back to Riverside and you didn't really find anything you were looking for."

My dad saw us now as he was leading an elderly woman down an aisle toward the organic toothpastes. He seemed mildly surprised but just smiled and waved. Good old Will.

"I don't know what I was looking for. It was a stupid idea and I felt worse after going."

"I know what you were looking for," Dean said.

"Yeah, me too," Gloria said.

"Guess that makes two out of three of us," I said, even more puzzled now.

"Can you take off from work?"

"Now?"

"Yes, now," Gloria said, her eyes intent.

"Sure," I said.

◄ ■ ►

We were rather quiet on the bus, the three of us. I asked Gloria about her parents but she said she was sick of thinking about them and didn't want to talk about it. And I decided not to open up the identity thing with Dean on the bus. He seemed pretty relaxed about himself right then. He had teamed up with Gloria to do this thing—for me. And I wasn't even sure I wanted to do it.

And then we were in Riverside.

"Where do you want to get off? Near the high school again?" Gloria asked.

I shook my head. "There'd be no point. No one would be there. Besides, I don't want to find Charlene again. Been there. Done that."

"Where then?"

"There's another park, about eight more blocks. My parents used to take me there."

Suddenly Gloria was not so certain this was a good idea. "Are you sure?"

"No," I said. "But we're here. You guys brought me here. We need to do something."

So we got off at the park. It was mostly empty. The grass was green and there were puddles in the playground area. We sat down on the swings—my dad used to give me a push and send me high up into the air. I pushed off and felt that familiar motion—the freedom of flight, even if it was just a few feet up into the air. I hadn't been on a swing since I'd left. I realized there were a lot of things I just stopped doing after that day long ago.

I wasn't sure this was a good idea. Maybe it was a very bad idea.

I jumped off the swing and walked over to the slide. It had seemed so big before. Now it was nothing. I took one rung at a time and went to the top. I remembered being here at this pinnacle as a small boy, maybe just six. I remember being scared. I made the slow descent to the bottom. Not much to it really, but long ago it had seemed thrilling. Dean followed after me as Gloria watched.

"What are we doing here?" I asked her, suddenly feeling both confused and angry. How could they possibly think they knew anything—anything at all—about what I had gone through and what I needed?

I was about to say we should leave and get the hell out of this town when I spotted something else. That spinning platform, a kind of merry-go-round thing that you powered by running and jumping on it. That had always been my favorite. I'd hang on for dear life as my father would run beside it, making the world go blurry, and I'd feel the centrifugal force trying to make me fly off into space. Then my dad would jump on, too, and he'd hang onto to me so I wouldn't fall. And my mom would be there—a blur, standing and smiling in the sun with each revolution, coming into and out of frame. And when you got off, the world was wobbling for a good solid minute until it settled itself down. And then we'd get our bearings and do it again and again.

I walked over to it and grabbed the metal handhold. I began to walk slowly beside it and then began to run. Gloria and Dean hung back and watched. I hopped on and made several slow revolutions. Then I jumped off and began to run beside it, holding on, making it go faster and faster, and finally I jumped on again and watched as the world began to blur around me. For a brief second, I was back there.

My father's arms were holding me in place. I looked straight forward, waiting for my mother to come into frame, but I couldn't find her. And then I let go, and the centrifugal spin threw me off so I landed hard on my butt and fell backwards onto the new grass. I lay there looking up at the blue spring sky and waited again for the world to stop spinning.

"Gotta hold on, dude," Dean said.

"You all right?" Gloria asked.

"Yeah." Nothing really hurt. I just didn't feel like getting up.

Dean sat down near me and Gloria lay down right alongside me and took my face in her hands, turned my head, and put her face up very close to mine so I could smell her warm, sweet breath. "You're not supposed to let go," she said. "Sometimes you have to hold on."

I wanted to kiss her but I felt self-conscious with Dean there. I also thought it might break the magic of whatever was happening here—the three of us as friends. Each of us with our own set of mysteries, our own problems, our own uncertainties.

I sat up. "Let's walk," I said. "I need to walk."

We left the park and I bought them both a coffee at a nearby Tim Hortons. We sat rather quietly and watched the older crowd in there—some sad, some happy. Some sitting alone with their thoughts, sipping from a cup. Something was forming in my head. I wondered why I'd been holding back. I wondered if Gloria and Dean were waiting for this.

When we finished, I said, "Come on. Let's go."

"Where?" Dean asked.

But Gloria understood. She just nodded.

◄ ■ ►

The house looked different from what I remembered. It was still a story and a half, a small house on a tidy piece of property. But the color of the house was blue now. It had been a kind of green when I was growing up. The shade of green of the spring grass in the park. Like everything else in town, it looked smaller as well.

"I'm going to knock on the door and see if they'll let me in," I said.

Dean looked shocked but Gloria understood. They hung back as I walked up my old driveway and along the short sidewalk leading to the front door. I kept all my emotions locked away deep within me right then. Otherwise, I could not have taken a single step. But I was here. I wanted to see what would happen.

I knocked on the door but there was no answer. I tried four times. No one was home. There was no car in the driveway.

But I felt like I had traveled a long, long journey to get here.

I had never even driven past here since I moved away.

I'd never come back to visit. I had just put it all behind me in the past. But now I felt different. I was aching to see the inside of the house. I opened the storm door and tried the door handle. It wasn't locked.

I turned the handle and opened the door.

And then I walked in.

The living room was to the left. I walked into it and it now seemed very familiar. I was in a safe, warm place. The furniture was different, as were the pictures on the wall, but the fireplace was still there. And I could almost see my mother reading in a pool of light. I could almost see the Stratocaster in its guitar stand by the corner. The shades were drawn so it was very dim inside. I did not turn on a light. I sat down on the carpet in the middle of the living room and took a deep breath. I closed my eyes and went back there.

It was night—maybe a month before the accident. My father had not yet quit his nighttime job at the 7-Eleven. My mother had let me stay up late and wait for him to come home. The house was quiet. So very quiet. I was sitting on the floor with a pile of comic books, reading one of my favorites for maybe the eighth time. And then my father came home. Henry walked in, kissed Seal, and handed her some ice cream he brought home for her and for me. I remember the book Seal was reading fell to the floor. I was truly back there. And at that point in my life everything—everything—was fine.

I don't know how long I sat there like that. I eventually heard the storm door open and Dean and Gloria both walked in.

"Joe, you gotta get out of here, man," Dean said.

I guess I didn't move or say anything because, after a minute, both Dean and Gloria were beside me. "Let me stay here for just a couple more minutes," I said.

Dean and Gloria looked at each other but said nothing more. Then they sat down on the floor beside me.

◄ ■ ►

And that's what the owner of the house saw when he walked in his own front door—the three of us sitting in the middle of his living room floor. I opened my eyes when I heard the voice. "What the hell is this?" he shouted.

He was about forty, a bit heavy. He had on clothes that suggested he worked on a construction site. In his arms was a bag of groceries.

"Drugs, right?" he said. "I'm calling the police."

But as he walked toward the kitchen to use the phone, we quickly vacated the premises.

When he noticed we were leaving, he ran out the front door after us but we had a good lead. And we had all three become like the wind. We ran until we could run no further. And if we hadn't started to laugh so hard, I might not have ended up crying. But cry I did.

CHAPTER SIXTEEN

DEAN E-MAILS ME MORE FROM THE DEAN'S LIST OF FAMOUS GAY people. Alexander the Great—the tyrant. Francis Bacon—the philosopher. Lord Byron and Walt Whitman—poets. Herman Melville, who wrote *Moby Dick*. Eleanor Roosevelt, who was married to a U.S. president. Tchaikovsky—the Russian composer. Martina Navratilova—the tennis star. Even Leonardo da Vinci and Michelangelo and Julius Caesar.

I don't know what his sources for this are. But somebody has him convinced all the above were gay. I believe it's possible. I just wonder what the evidence is. What is exactly recorded in history about Alexander the Great, for example, that lets us know he was homosexual? Did someone write it on the wall in an ancient outhouse? Did Alex announce it to his troops one day? I mean, if an author writes something autobiographical about his or her sexual persuasion, that makes sense. But history is a funny place. So I just don't know.

Now, before anyone starts calling me homophobic, I'm just trying to remind you I hold a healthy skepticism about everything. Everything.

Dean's other list that followed in a second e-mail included all the slang terms he could locate for gay men. He said he

133

was just preparing himself for whatever might be thrown at him. I will spare you the list. Some were insulting. Some were funny. Some slightly endearing. The Australian one, however, stood out. A gay surfer in Australia might be called a "Nancy boy" if he showed his gayness while out amongst his mates, sitting in the ocean on his surfboard. Depending on how you took this, it might not be that cruel at all. And, just for the record, if anyone is listening, Dean's mental jury is still out as to whether he really is gay or not. I have a feeling he is not going to resolve this one easily. I'm his sounding board, though, so I will keep you up to date.

But I digress. And I digress because I am thinking of the living room scene a while back. I digress because I have yet to process that and because I think it is a step along a path that I am not sure I am ready to take. I did not tell Will and Beth about it. I think it might scare them. It could make them think I still want my old parents back (and I do) but that might hurt their feelings. They could think I am rejecting them. (And I am not.) I just want to bring my first parents back from the dead. I really do. I want a full resurrection. I want that.

But I remain skeptical that any of this adds up to anything. Do you know what a true skeptic is? It is a follower of yet another Greek philosopher, not quite of Aristotle's rank, but a fine intellect, nonetheless. And no, he was not named Skepticle. His name was Pyrrho of Elis. He and his students down through the moldering centuries doubt that it is possible to acquire real knowledge of any sort. They feel that there are no adequate grounds for the existence of truth of any kind. The word itself comes from the Greek meaning to "look around" or to "observe."

Just one cold, hard look at the world is enough to send you off to join the legion of Pyrrho. Just join the parade.

We use the word somewhat differently today and usually it means someone who doubts things. I am both a skeptic and a doubter. But I am also apparently my own hero with a thousand faces, which is why I may confuse you so much. Say one thing, do another. Of course, how human of me. The "skeptick," as Sir Walter Raleigh once noted, "doth neither affirm or neither denie any position." Walt said this was a bad thing. This from a man who gave England—and hence the rest of the world—tobacco to be smoked and, ultimately, cigarettes. Think of the generations to whom he gave the gift of lung cancer. Had he been more of a skeptic, he would not have believed that the tobacco given him by Virginia native folk was a health remedy. A skeptical Raleigh might have saved us a lot of grief.

Which leads, of course, to the notion that belief leads to action whereas doubt leads to inaction. These are my musings at the end of a week without school. A week that turned into a kind of quest. Maybe the truly important truths of life are (to use Joe Campbell's word) "unknowable." But if that is the case, why do we keep seeking answers and connections?

And that, dear diary, is what this diary is all about. It seems I can travel in any direction—mentally or physically—and discover something. But it is not always forward. It is forward, then backward, into the future, and then into the past. And all the while making tangential side trips. Places. Theories. Names.

◄ ■ ►

I admit to some disappointment about the Joe list—famous men named Joe, that is. Certainly, it is not as interesting or formidable as the Dean's List. But I'm pleased with my connection to this Joseph Campbell guy. It seems that he was actually misquoted somewhere—supposedly saying something like: each of us should be following our own "bliss." Oh, boy. He was talking about a character from a book, unhappy because he did not follow his bliss. Bliss as in happiness. How can you follow it if you don't know what it looks like? If I can find mine, I may try to follow it, but it seems that, by going back to Riverside, my quest was to follow my own unhappiness. Perhaps we cannot let go of our past. We must always go back. Even if it is painful.

And that took me on another tangent. Had a slow first day back at school. Everyone kind of wonky—students and teachers—about being back in harness. Me just a bit dazed. Deaner seeming not so fidgety. Gloria looking okay in a medicated sort of way. I thanked them both for the trip down memory lane. I apologized about the crying. When I had cried, they both cried, too—Dean a little, Gloria a lot. All of us taking off our masks at once. Wow.

So school was just school and I started thinking about last names. Born a Campbell. What exactly did that mean? Hadn't I kept my names, both first and last when adopted? I must have thought it meant something to keep the name I was born with and not become a MacDonald like my current parents. There had been talk of hyphenation. Joseph Campbell-MacDonald. Kind of like soup and hamburger. It may have hurt Will and Beth's feelings, but I did not want to be a hyphenated boy. It just didn't feel right.

I was dawdling in a study period in the library, walking among the shelves, when I closed my eyes and pulled a book at random from the shelves. An old book about the history of Scotland—of which I must say I knew very little. I opened to a random page and discovered that there was something there about the "Clan Campbell." We had a clan?

All right, so I discover that my name is of Scottish origin. No one ever told me that. So now I have roots. I find a seat at an empty table and, suddenly, I am tossed back into the quagmire that is the history of the people who once shared my family name. These are my ancestors.

I learned that Clan Campbell was an ancient Celtic family traced back to Colin Mor Campbell, who was killed (there was a lot of bloodshed in those days) in 1294. Campbell means, get this, "a wry or twisted mouth" in Gaelic. Not exactly something to be proud of. (I looked later in the boys' bathroom mirror at my mouth and decided it was neither wry nor twisted, traits apparently bred out of the Campbells down through the generations.)

It gets worse, though. Not better. We Campbells were a nasty, churlish lot, it seems. The name has been hated by many—especially, it turns out, by the MacDonalds—right up to today. No kidding. I'd be better off changing my last name if I was to tour around Scotland. And for good reason. Here's why.

There was feuding between families—between clans. Way, way back, the Campbell folk supported a leader named Robert the Bruce who dominated most of Scotland in the fourteenth century, and he had to continually battle the clans who did not like him. The MacDonalds, for example, were enemies of the Bruces. Keep in mind that, as usual, religion got its thorny barbs into all this. The Bruces and Campbells were Protestant and a lot of other clans like the MacDonalds, especially in the Highlands, were Catholic. Many small clans were literally annihilated by the Campbell warriors. Wholesale slaughter was part of the Campbell family tradition. The book added that the Campbells' "persecution of the MacGregors, in particular, leaves a stench behind."

So, fast forward to the seventeenth century where the Campbell folk did one decidedly nasty deed that left an even bigger stink down through the centuries. The Campbells, by then, had sworn loyalty to the English—King William of Orange, to be specific. The MacDonalds wanted nothing to do with the English.

A contingent of Campbell men was sent by the king to the Highland village of Glencoe in the winter of 1692, supposedly to collect taxes. Strangely enough, the MacDonalds in Glencoe offered food and shelter that bitter cold and sleety February to the Campbells. After two weeks of this good hospitality, the Campbells turned on their hosts (as they had been instructed to) at five AM one morning and murdered the Glencoe MacDonalds.

Thirty-eight unsuspecting men were massacred, and forty other MacDonald women and children died afterwards from freezing and starvation as they fled.

And so it is, ages hence, that an orphaned Campbell boy, his own parents dead as the result of faulty brake lights, is adopted and taken into the home of a MacDonald family. What do you make of that, I ask you, in this riddled random universe?

And that's all I have to say about that. School again tomorrow. Big test in biology. Boy to bed. Over and out.

CHAPTER SEVENTEEN

PART OF ME WAS STILL STUCK BACK THERE IN MY OLD LIVING ROOM. It really was. I gave in and tried to talk to Will and Beth about it. They tried to help me but it was awkward. "You can talk to us about anything," my mom said.

"We're here for you," my dad said. "Just let us know what you need."

That didn't make it any easier. Maybe what I needed was the nasty version of parents. The ones who would say, "Get over it." But I didn't have the get-over-it type of parents. I changed the subject and asked them if they ever heard about the Campbell-MacDonald issue. They hadn't. But that, too, was a piece of the puzzle. My puzzle. And oh, yeah, here I go again. The puzzle of me. What do I mean? Who am I? What do the events of my life add up to? If it really was a puzzle, there would always be pieces, big pieces, missing. So, get over that, too.

Still, with a name like mine, I must be on a quest. All I have are clues. Many of which do not add up. So what does a boy do but follow some deep, primitive need, some instinct, maybe?

None of which was helping Gloria. And she did need help. I skipped class and went looking for her. She was not in school—again. I phoned. Nothing. I asked Dean if he'd seen her. He hadn't.

Field notes on the Deanster, by the way. His jury is still out on the gay guy thing. But, he now has four gay friends. Two guys—Tim and Devon—and two girls—Lee Anne and Clarisse. They've kind of adopted him. Dean likes that. He seems more relaxed and at home in his Deanness, gay or straight. His uncertainty about his sexual persuasion has vastly improved his social life. Go figure.

But Gloria. Gloria was not in Excelsis. Gloria, I discovered, was in the Children's Hospital. I stopped by her house after school. There were both of Gloria's parents together, answering the door.

"The meds were not working," her mom said somberly.

"We had to help her somehow," her dad added. They were unhappy parents but they did not seem like they were unhappy with each other.

"Can I see her?" I asked.

Her mom looked at me rather severely. "She says you two slept together. Is that true?"

"Yes," I said rather matter-of-factly. "So can I see her? Is she here?"

"She's in the Children's Hospital."

"What?" I asked, feeling the blood drain from my face.

"It was what her doctor recommended," her dad said, looking now like an entirely defeated man.

"She's just depressed," her mom added, making it sound like she had a cold.

"Very depressed," her father added. "And it's our fault."

"Don't say that," her mom said, with an edge to her voice.

"I know she's been hurting," I said. "I thought I could help. Maybe I still can."

"I don't know," her father said. "Might be best to let the doctors do what they can."

But I already knew where she was. Sounded odd. But I guess they put kids in a "children's hospital" right up until they turn seventeen.

Mom disagreed with Dad again. "I think he should go see her."

Dad shrugged, didn't want to argue.

"I'll call ahead," Gloria's mom said, "and tell them it's all right for you to visit. Room 354. Follow the blue line on the floor."

I hadn't been in the Children's Hospital since ... well, since I'd been a child. I'd fallen off my bike when I was eight and had a bad cut on my leg that wouldn't stop bleeding. It took some stitches and some hollering on my part to get through it. My parents bought me ice cream afterwards. Bubble-gum-flavored ice cream that I later threw up on a beige carpet. Do you have any idea what bubble gum ice cream vomit does to beige? I do.

Sure enough, there was a blue line on the floor as soon as you walked in. And it led to the third floor—the psychiatric ward, I supposed, although they didn't have that posted anywhere. No one asked me who I was or anything. I just walked to 354. The door was open. I knocked anyway on the frame.

Gloria was fully dressed and sitting in a chair by the window. She was reading.

She looked up. She seemed happy to see me but even the half-smile couldn't mask the injured look in her eyes.

"What are you reading?" I asked.

"*One Hundred Years of Solitude*," she said.

"That sounds cheery."

"It's good. Gabriel Garcia Marquez. He's from South America."

"I always liked South American authors," I said.

"Liar."

I smiled. So did she. Not much of one. But a smile.

"You okay?" I asked.

"I'm here. How can I be okay?"

"Right. What do they do for you here?"

"They talk to me."

"That's all."

"So far."

"But why are you here?"

"I couldn't find the courage to go to school."

"You didn't want to go to school? Big deal."

"I *couldn't* get up for school."

"Did it have something to do with me? That whole scene in Riverside?"

"Maybe. But that was maybe just what triggered it. I just woke up and didn't feel like moving. I didn't feel like doing anything. I had fallen into a very deep, very dark pit. And I had no desire to try to climb out."

"I talked to your parents."

"They're back together."

"I noticed."

"They are doing that for me. I don't know if it's going to work. Believe it or not, they're talking about staying in the same house—my mom upstairs, my dad in the basement. There's a bedroom and bathroom there and he's talking about putting in a kitchen. They think they need to do this for me."

"Can it work?"

"I doubt it. But I feel guilty that I'm making things worse for them—with all this."

"Guilt is a waste of time," I said, suddenly flashing on something. Something big. I shoved it back into a closet.

"I don't think they can help me," Gloria said, nodding at the busy staff people out at the nurse's station.

"Don't say that."

Gloria shrugged. "I'll stay here for a while. Gives me time to read. I don't care about school."

"You ever feel this bad before?"

"Yeah. A few times. Growing up. I'd fall into the pit but could always get back out. This is different."

"Deeper pit?"

"Something like that."

"When you look up, what do you see?"

She set her book down and looked directly at me. "I see you leaning over. You're yelling something to me but I can't hear it."

"You're sure it's me?"

"Yes. And I'm yelling to you to be careful. Not to lean over too far. I'm afraid you might fall."

"I won't fall," I said.

I came closer to Gloria and touched her cheek with my hand. She held it there and I felt important and helpless all at the same time.

After that, I told her about Dean and about my research into the Campbells and the MacDonalds. She was pleased about Dean and somewhat disturbed by the activities of my ancestors.

And then one of the nurses was telling me visiting hours were over. "I'll be back," I told Gloria. "I'll come every day." But the truth was that being around Gloria, seeing the dark look in her eyes, the sadness, was not good. As I left the room, I felt relieved. As I left the hospital, I felt free. All my good intentions were flushed down a toilet. All I could think about was getting away from there. So I found myself running down the endless sidewalk until my lungs felt like they were on fire. I let myself fall over on someone's lawn and lay there, breathing hard, having a hard time getting the picture of Gloria's sorrowful face out of my head.

I knew then that I wasn't strong enough to help her. I felt really rotten. A loser, a failure, a fraud. I stumbled on back home and locked myself in my room.

I fell asleep and didn't wake up from some truly bad dreams until somewhere around midnight. The knocking mixed into what I was dreaming. It was the police knocking at the door to the house. Coming to report what happened to Henry and Seal. But, as I awoke to darkness, I realized where I was and that it was just Will and Beth.

I got out of bed and opened the door. Something harsh but important was forming in my thoughts.

"We heard you shouting something in your sleep," Beth said. "Are you all right?"

I rubbed my eyes and tried to hang onto what my brain was screaming at me. I'm sure I looked very confused.

"Yeah. I think I am. I think I know what I have to do."

CHAPTER EIGHTEEN

BEFORE I TELL YOU ABOUT WHAT HAPPENED TODAY, I CONFESS THAT I am still shaking. It may take me a few days to calm down. Maybe a month. Maybe it's going to take me a lifetime. Why I had the courage to do it today, I'm not sure. Something to do with Gloria. Seeing her in the state she was in. Realizing that the medication and probably even the professional staff at the hospital were not going to be able to help her. I was the only one who could climb down into the darkness and help her find a way up.

I know what you must be thinking. Boy with a hero complex. Only *he* can save the girl.

Yes. That's exactly what I was thinking. Is that so foolish of me? But first, I knew I had to face my own demons. Not demons, really. Just memory. And not really even memory. Images of something I did not see, even though I lived it over and over a thousand times.

I told no one what I was up to. All I had to do was go there.

I could try to give you some reasonable psychological explanation about why I was going there today, this otherwise nondescript Saturday in my life. But I won't. You connect the dots. If the dots connect at all. It's better that way. I'll just report the events.

Here goes.

I got up and I brushed my teeth, put on jeans, a long sleeve T-shirt, socks, and running shoes. Will and Beth weren't up, so I left them a note. "Out for a bit. Will be back later," it said. Vague and ordinary. But brave, really. Very brave. Was it the Campbell in me or the MacDonald? Certainly the sound in my head was the guitar. Henry's full-throttle distortion guitar—one big monster chord. But I was also feeling Will's confidence and sense of purpose. When he knew a thing had to be done, he just set himself to do it. No complaining, no matter how menial or tedious or difficult. With those two fathers in my head, I truly felt hyphenated.

But this wasn't really about fathers. This was about me. And, of course, it was about the boy on the bicycle.

So what else? After the note, I left the house, caught the now familiar bus to Riverside. I don't remember anything at all about the bus ride. Honest. No faces, no sounds. Nothing.

But I did know where to get off.

I got off at the exact location where my mom and dad were killed. I knew where it was. The corner of Memorial Highway and Silver Street. After the accident, I never once went to visit this place where they died. I'd driven past there with Will or Beth, but no one said a word, and I would turn my eyes up to the sky rather than focus on that corner.

The Memorial part of the highway name had to do with dead soldiers, I think. I don't know why Silver Street was named that. Why silver? Why not gold or platinum?

I got off the bus and just stood there on the sidewalk. The highway was busy. Cars were moving pretty fast. There were a lot of trucks. Silver Street had a stop sign. I stared at that for a while, wondered how long it had been here. Cars were supposed to stop on Silver Street and wait for a break in traffic before getting onto Memorial Highway. You could only turn right. If you wanted to go left on Memorial, you would have to approach on another street. This did not look like a particularly dangerous intersection.

Time seemed to have stopped. I looked up at the sky first. It was empty and pale blue, like the color of a robin's egg. I looked around at the houses. Perfectly ordinary houses. There was a tree in the yard of the closest house. A maple tree, dropping those little helicopter seed pods that were spinning down from the leaves. I decided I liked the maple tree. It was an old, solid-looking tree and it would have been here the night they died. One of them might have noticed it, I thought, although it was getting dark then and maybe they didn't see it at all. I just like to think that they did and that now I was admiring the same tree. A connection.

I stared at the links in the chain-link fence along the sidewalk. The fence that separated a small, rather shabby baseball field from the highway. The fence was somewhat rusty and bent down a bit in places. It looked like people must have been climbing over it, but I don't know why anyone would do that, when you could just walk around it easily enough there, at the corner of Silver Street.

The sidewalk took my attention for a while. Concrete. Chewing gum smushed into it in places, by people standing there waiting for the bus. No one else was standing here now, waiting. The next bus was probably a long way off.

There were cracks in the concrete—random patterns. Nothing special. Nothing important.

I started to wonder how long I'd have to stay here. What exactly was I expecting to happen?

I took a picture out of my wallet. Henry, Seal, and me. I must have been about ten in the picture. The sun was in my eyes and I was squinting. Henry and Seal were looking at the camera. I don't know where the photo was taken. I just remember that my mom had asked a stranger to take the picture. The two adults in the photo seemed very familiar and very close to me. What I mean is that it seemed like I'd been with them yesterday or the day before. Like they had never gone away. But the boy in the photo appeared to me as a complete stranger.

Had I ever really been the boy in that photo? Maybe the kid was just a stand-in. Two adults asking a random kid to have his photo taken with them. Maybe.

An older teenage couple walked by me then. They were holding hands and laughing. Boy and a girl. Pierced lip on the girl. Pierced eyebrow on the guy. They looked at me and nodded. Maybe they thought I was waiting for the bus. I was inconsequential to them, and suddenly I thought it amazing that people could look at me, right here, at this important moment in my life, this powerfully significant location, and *not* know what was going on in my head.

I looked at the oncoming traffic. A constant flow. Cars passing. All flowing smoothly. Nobody on Silver Street seemed the slightest bit interested in driving to the stop sign and then entering the highway. Silver Street was quiet and empty. I peered down this empty street and suddenly caught the glimpse of something shiny. A little kid on a bike—just a split second image of him turning into a driveway, and then he was gone.

And then I looked back at the stop sign. I felt myself being swallowed by a cold wave of something that consumed me from head to toe. The boy on the bike. They had said he was about eleven or twelve. My age at the time. There had been, the police said, this boy on a bike who must have gone through the stop sign, recklessly heading out into the traffic, directly in front of my parents. And as Henry had slammed on his brakes, the garbage truck driver behind him did not react quickly enough. There had been no brake lights. Nothing.

The boy had been spared. He had veered quickly away and then left the scene immediately. Vanished. He did not want to be blamed. I'm guessing at this but all the police could say was that someone had seen a boy on a bike, had witnessed him ride quickly away. Quickly away, I assume, into his own ordinary life, with his two ordinary parents. Quite possibly he did not tell them. He kept his secret, lest he be blamed.

Now I know this next part is going to sound crazy, totally insane. But hear me out. I had arrived in my mind at my destination. Not just Memorial Highway and Silver Street but at the very time of the accident as well. But the perspective was wrong. I needed to be there on the highway, not just here on the sidewalk. I'd seen the photograph. It had appeared in the paper. It had been taken after the bodies had been removed. A rear-ended car. Crushed from behind. Glass all over the highway.

My father must have kept his foot well planted on the brake pedal. The car had not been pushed very far—just across the width of Silver Street—and it stayed there right on the highway.

But directly in front of me was where the impact would have occurred. There was a break in traffic and I stepped out onto the asphalt of the right-hand lane. I looked directly ahead now and envisioned the boy on the bike. I imagined him approaching in the dim light of evening. He was going way too fast and he was reckless, for sure. What was he thinking about that would allow him to ride right out into the traffic? Did he think he saw an opening between cars that he could have slipped through? Did he think he was going to ride right across the highway and not get hurt? I tried to get his face into focus by squinting my eyes like the boy in the wallet photograph.

And then I recognized who it was. The boy that I imagined on the bike was me.

And what had I been thinking, stepping out into the flow of traffic myself just then? Did I think the drivers would just steer around me? But time had stopped. And I was seeing what my father and mother had seen just before the garbage truck made impact. I was looking at the swerving boy on the bike.

One driver lay hard on his horn, slipped over into the passing lane and never slowed at all. I tried to move my legs. I honestly tried but they would not move. I could twist my neck around and see the oncoming cars. It was an open, straight stretch of highway. The driver of each speeding car seemed to take the lead from the one before it, realize something or someone was in the lane ahead, and they inched their way over and just kept going.

I could turn now, fully around, facing the traffic, strangely fascinated by the fact that I had this power to make all those drivers move over. I heard their car horns and saw their angry faces as they passed. More than one driver yelled something but I couldn't make out the words.

But there was one car that was different. It did not move over into the passing lane and it was headed straight toward me. A woman was driving. She was talking on a cell phone. She was distracted. I could see her face clearly by the time she saw me. She dropped her phone and slammed on her brakes. I watched the car hurtling toward me but it was like in the movies—slow motion. I tried again to make my legs move, but they did not. I heard the squeal of the tires. I smelled the burning rubber.

And then it stopped.

I fell to my knees and lowered my head.

The woman got out of the car and began to scream at me. No one else stopped. The traffic continued to simply move over into the passing lane and kept going. "Get up!" the woman shouted. "You could have been killed. Are you crazy?"

I looked up at her then and watched her angry face shift ever so slowly to something else. She saw something in my eyes. She looked frantically around, realizing the danger we were both in. She grabbed my arm with a fierce grip. "Get in the car," she said, lifting me.

I did as she said. I got in the car. She turned the corner onto Silver Street and pulled over to the side of the road after we were well away from the highway. Without saying a word, she got out of the car again and sat down on the grass by the curb. When I got out and walked over to her, I said, "I'm so sorry." But I could not begin to explain to her why I'd done something so crazy. I just kept repeating, "I'm sorry,

I'm sorry." She had her head down now and was crying. My own tears did not come.

A few neighbors were watching, but no one seemed to want to get involved. I knew the smart thing to do would have been to get away from there before someone phoned the police. All I had to do was run. Just disappear. But I thought about the boy on the bike again. So I stayed.

I sat down on the curb beside the crying woman and I put my arm around her. She didn't pull away. I felt responsible for her pain and expected her to get angry at me any second and start screaming at me. But she didn't.

Eventually, she turned to me, wiped away her tears, and just looked up into my eyes. She must have seen my own fear, my confusion, and my pain. "Are you all right?" she finally asked.

"Yeah. You?"

"I will be," she said, her whole body shaking now. "You want to tell me what that was about?"

I figured I had no choice. I owed her that much. I told her my story. Then she said her name was Marie and she asked me where I lived. I told her. And then she offered to drive me home and I accepted. She was maybe forty years old, a mother of twin boys who were eight. But she said her third child, a girl, died not long after she was born and she'd never been quite the same since. She didn't tell me her last name or where she lived. When she dropped me off at my house, she asked again if I was going to be okay. I said yes and I apologized yet one more time.

◄ ■ ►

And now I'm back in my room. Will and Beth have gone out food shopping. I will probably not tell them any of this. Just for the record, I, of course, was not really the boy on the bike that day. I was home working on my homework, as you recall. But for a long, long time, I must have dreamed it or imagined it and lived with it in my head. I identified with that damn kid on the bike. And I had blamed myself for the death of Henry and Seal. And when I discovered I could not live with the ferocity of that blame, once I had moved on to new parents and a new home, I had said goodbye to Joey-1, to Joseph One, and become Joe—Joseph Two. And, quite possibly, that had been a mistake.

CHAPTER NINETEEN

I HAVE A THEORY. AND THE THEORY IS THIS. FOR EVERY THEORY, THERE is an equal and opposite theory. And I know you are probably more interested in hearing more about the boy who was standing in the highway than the one sitting here talking into the microphone of his digital diary right now, but my diary days are numbered. In fact, I think they are just about over. But the Joe Campbell sitting in this room now is tossing about a few ideas. Tossing about futures. Tossing about visions of his past.

In ancient Greece, according to my Mom's old *OED*, a theor was an ambassador sent to a foreign country to consult an oracle. An oracle was someone who could see into the future. The theor would go find the seer and bring home the news to his king, be it good or ill. A theory was a whole delegation of theors, since apparently it sometimes required more than one man to carry the weight of the future back to the homeland.

Later, in English, a "theory" grew to mean a possible explanation for why things are the way they are. Sometimes the theory is based on hard empirical evidence, upon experiments and rigorous testing. Sometimes a theory can be pure speculation. In either case, sometimes a theory proves true, sometimes false. Sometimes it appears to be true for hundreds of years until a new explanation comes along. A better one, a more provable one that will again, one day further into the future, be deemed untrue.

Sometimes, an open-minded person (like myself, for example) can hold two opposing theories in his head at the same time. Possibly even believe both of them, despite the fact that it is illogical to believe in A and also in its opposite, B, at the same time. I still believe that I myself have been conjured up by this random universe through a random set of events, and yet, as I have traveled back into resolving the crisis of the two Josephs, I discover odd linkages, patterns, if you will.

And therein lies, possibly, meaning.

The boy on the bike is still me. Is now and forever more. I cannot fully forgive myself for the death of my parents. (Don't tell me this is not logical. It's just the way it is.) But I've reconnected with the twelve-year-old. (And yes, I realize it was not really me but some other cowardly, unnamed boy who sped away that day on his bike, unscathed but not, I dare say, unwounded.) And both boys remind me that there is another pilgrimage I must make soon. To the gravesite where I have not been since the day of the funeral. I think I'll give that some more time yet. I've gathered up the courage for Charlene, for the living room, and then for the corner of Memorial Highway and Silver Street. I need a bit more time yet for the journey to their resting place. And once I am there, I want it to be a beginning of something, not an end.

I never did get the full story of Marie. I expect I will never see her again. But there was something that happened there that meant something to her. My stupidity had an effect on her life, possibly a life-changing one. She knows where I live. Perhaps someday she will stop to tell me what else went on in her head that Saturday. Perhaps not. I just know that there will be other strangers in my life who will help me. And I will be on the lookout for them.

Whoever you are, reading this, fear not. I will not go looking for another close call with death again. I didn't really go looking for that at all. Let's say that it just happened. I am through with standing in highways. Been there. Done that.

Back to my two theories. Nothing happens for a purpose. Everything happens for a purpose. Equal and opposite. I'm sorry, but that's the way I see it. Even when something has no meaning, no meaningful directed series of events, there is a result.

◄ ■ ►

I thought that last entry would be the final one. But I guess I was wrong. It's been a while since then, but tonight I had this feeling I should make one further report.

I told my parents I want the hyphenation of my name. Maybe not right now. But the year I graduate from high school. I want to become Joseph Campbell-MacDonald and then travel around Scotland for the summer. I'm curious to see how people in Scotland will react. I'll take a guitar with me and a book or two of poetry. And if all goes well, Gloria will join me. I've already told her about the plan. She's skeptical but I have time yet to convince her. I'll make sure we eat well as we travel, stopping to buy organic food from health food stores and farmers. And on occasion, if I can get up the courage, I'll stop on a city street and read poetry out loud as I play guitar, and people will throw some change in my guitar case. Gloria and I will sleep in hostels and visit ancient pagan sites of standing stones.

But that's a long way off.

I'm working with the random clues now. I open my mother's old *OED* to any page and let my eye fall on whatever word is there. Today it is the word "comprehend," which once meant to overtake and now means to "grasp with the mind," or "to know a thing as well as that thing can be known," as the poet John Donne says.

And there is certainly a lot of grasping going on in my mind. A lot of holding on.

I am still holding on to Gloria. She is out of the hospital but still taking medication. Her parents are attempting to live together. Dad in the basement, Mom upstairs. Gloria is, I think, being held as an emotional hostage between them. She's back in school but not out of the woods yet, as they say. She comes to my house and sleeps with me each Saturday night. I hold her and, no, we still don't have sex. But someday. Maybe. Not now.

I'm sure that appears very odd to those that know that we are sleeping together. My parents seem to have adjusted. Gloria's parents are confused by it, uncertain. But Gloria insists.

I miss the old Gloria. I miss the spark. I'm hoping it will return. These things take time.

She works with me at the health food store on weekends. (Yes, we're even open Sundays.) I've counseled her in glucosamine and amino acids, flax seed oil, and luten. She's learned the ropes quickly and we make a good team.

But I know what you are thinking.

This all seems a little bit too tidy. And that is not necessarily the way life is.

◄ ■ ▶

x marks the spot. At any given moment in our lives, we are at a crossroads, an intersection of past and present. This is where I am now, digital diary. I am still a boy of sixteen years of age. Confused but purposeful. The story so far, as they say, is now contained. It is an artifact. It will end soon (as you can tell). I'm trying a bit too hard to end it, to leave it with an ending. But there is none.

If all the audio files were etched onto a memory chip and sent into deep space, what would those potential sentient aliens who decode it think of me? What would they make of my life? Would I be the hero with the thousand faces, or just an orphaned and adopted boy, floundering in his own life?

I expect the floundering to continue. How could it not?

But something is different. Much different. I am a prize package of contradictions and will leave it at that.

As I stumble to my close here, I feel some sadness. I thought I might ultimately share this diary with my father who inspired it, and my mother as well. But I will not. They would only worry about me more.

And I had fancied that I would turn it over to Gloria, that she was my perfect audience. But I don't think I will do that. I will help her wrestle with her own demons but need not ask her to come rescue me from mine. Not now, anyway.

She still falls into darkness from time to time, but she tells me that she can always see my face, no matter how deep, how dark. I am no hero, however. I answer the phone when it rings at one-thirty in the morning. I talk to her. And one night a week, I hold her.

And you must be wondering about Dean. I'm pleased to report that Dean is still Dean, although somewhat improved. He has not come any closer to concluding whether he is gay or straight, but he has several gay friends, guys and girls. He seems happier, less confused, despite his ... well ... confusion, on that issue. Dean will always be my friend, and I like it that he leans less on me now.

◄ ■ ►

I tried to sleep but I couldn't. So I guess I'm back. An Ordinary Joe. Joe Schmo, with a footnote to everything I've said.

In physics, I have learned in my random quest for knowledge, there is something called the theory of everything. It is referred to as a theorist's "dream" because the theory of everything does not currently exist. But it could exist. It is hinted at in another theory called the grand unified theory that involves a lot of talk about quarks and leptons and gluons. It involves notions about minuscule bits of matter and force-carrying particles. Matter and energy. And no, I don't really know what I'm talking about here. I just hope that the theory of everything, should it ever come into being, will include room for me, and for Gloria and for Dean, and my two sets of parents, one living, one dead—and for a woman named Marie. And it should include the boy on the bike. Matter and energy. And one lone voice speaking into a digital recorder. A story told that will, one day, far off from today, have an audience. And that audience will be me.

INTERVIEW WITH
LESLEY CHOYCE

What triggered this story for you?

I had heard so many people using the word "random" in recent years although the very meaning of it had become, well, random. And I was, yet again, trying to sort out whether my own life made sense, whether there was a true purpose that we all have or if the events of our lives are haphazard and hence random.

So I came up with Joey and his own personal dilemma. His was, I admit, a bit deeper and darker than my own. I wanted a different kind of narrative, one that was fragmented and yet compelling, which is the way most of us think. That's why I used the digital diary idea. Once Joey got going with his DD, of course, he took over and all I had to do was hang on and follow his random thoughts and struggles to prove there is no meaning or purpose to life while being gobsmacked over and over with indications that it does all add up to something. Something of great significance.

The young men in your young adult novels are intelligent, sensitive, well-read. It's refreshing to find books which set aside some of the common misconceptions about teenage boys. Can you comment on that?

Everyone I have ever known is unique and eccentric in their own way. I want Joey and my other male teen characters to exemplify teenage boys who have very complex emotional and intellectual lives. I was certainly not ever normal in my teen years. No one is. Most teenage guys are actually quite sensitive, intelligent, and fragile. The young macho stuff is just a facade in almost all cases. The massive force of social conditioning that comes today mostly from commercialism and pop culture deprives many teens from exploring their own unique identity. So it is my hope that my quirky characters resonate for both guys and girls and encourages them to be who they want to be. I've received enough e-mails from readers of my books to know that, for some, these novels do connect and help liberate the spirit of those struggling to figure out who they are, those suffering from "being different," those who feel alienated and isolated.

When you first named your protagonist Joe Campbell, did you know you were going to reveal to him the book by the other Joseph Campbell?

That was a fluke. All I knew was that his name was Joe, then Joey. At first, I wanted to usher in some Scottish history, of all things. I had been reading about the feuds and warfare between the Campbells and the MacDonalds. And then it occurred to me that Joey's formal name was Joseph Campbell, the author whose books I had read in university. I had an "aha" moment or two over that and when I did a bit more research into the life and work of Joseph Campbell, I realized there were some extremely interesting connections to my character and his dilemma. It was then that I was reminded of the fact that there were some rather significant forces of creative energy outside of me that were helping to shape this book.

Joe begins as a boy who is profoundly confused about the purpose of life, because of what has happened to him. But would you agree that this is a condition that applies to most teens at some point in their lives? And is it a handicap for them?

Hey, not just teens. I am still profoundly befuddled and confused about many things. And yet the confusion and uncertainty, I've found, is really the wellspring of my curiosity and creativity. I don't know if I have a purpose in life, and if I was certain of it, I would be a very different person. I live by my hunches and I think Joey is doing that too. When he discovers a hunch of his is wrong, he gets a bit more confused, but then absorbs the new information and moves on, or at least tries to. And thus he grows, matures. But there is no final absolute solution to his problem or an ultimate answer.

If you were to ask me what my own hunches are about what I'm doing on this planet, why I am here, I'd say this: I'm supposed to be creative and to write. I need to be kind and compassionate to everyone around me (including my enemies if I have any) as often as I can. I must absolutely give back more than I take. I must try my best to be honest with myself and with everyone around me even when it is difficult. I need to be daring and take chances (but not all the time). And I need to remain passionate about what I do and how I live. And I need to have some degree of fun while doing all the above.

Joe, Gloria, and Dean are outsiders in their world. You seem to write a lot about outsiders in your young adult novels. What qualities do such people have that make them interesting characters to build a story around?

When we are totally comfortable in our lives, our families, our jobs, and our communities, we feel safe and secure. We are comfortable insiders—inside such a nice, cozy (but almost always temporary) womb. It's a wonderful place to be; it's just that it doesn't work out that way all of the time. So then we become outsiders.

When you are young, you feel like an outsider because you are not fully fledged as an adult. You are simply too young. Then you become an adult and realize that you are still an outsider on a lot of levels. Outsiders are edgy, nervous, problematic, and interesting. They often don't know who they are but they know who they are not. Outsiders are still searching for identity and meaning and that makes them more interesting to write about.

As you develop a story for teenagers, setting doesn't seem to be of prime significance for you; the stories—and *Random* is an example—could take place anywhere in North America. Is this a deliberate approach?

I've written a number of novels that are very precisely set in Halifax and on the Eastern Shore of Nova Scotia where I live. Other novels, like *Random*, could happen in a random suburban community just about anywhere in North America. I think this makes it easy for many readers to imagine that the story is set in the town where they live. But then within that framework, the world of the narrator, Joey in this case, is fairly precise. It's primarily the landscape of his interior geography that is most important and that's where the reader should be. Travelling around inside Joey's head with him and living his life vicariously.

Random is a novel that focuses largely on the main character's thinking through his situation, rather than working out his problem with lively action. This demonstrates your respect for the reader, I think. Could you comment on this?

I think that most of us live our primary lives inside our heads. We work out most of our problems and make our discoveries internally although they may be triggered by external factors. The wonderful illusion of good first-person fiction is that you, the reader, become the character while you are reading. That is intended to be my "gift" to the reader. You pick up my book about a character who has never existed and events that have never happened. You accept the psychological game that I've created—the contract between reader and writer which is the agreement that the fiction is real, at least while you are reading the book. I can't waste the reader's time ... or mine. So I owe the reader the best possible world I can give him or her. Sometimes that is a daunting task. Fortunately for me, I let Joey take over the novel quite early on and all I had to do was follow his lead.

AUTHOR'S NOTE ABOUT THE DEDICATION

My 31-year-old daughter, Sunyata Choyce, works in South Africa as director of a charitable organization she created called Project COLORS International. On February 18, 2010, she was wading in the Indian Ocean at a beach in the town of Klein Krans with some local children. Along that stretch of coast, the beach is rather steep and the currents in the ocean can be treacherous.

Sunyata got caught in a rip current while she was in the water and was quickly pulled out to sea. The children made it safely to shore but Sunyata was swept away from the shoreline and was desperately in need of assistance. At first, no one could hear her yelling for help.

Fortunately, two shark fishermen, Jacques Starbuck and Jacques Snyman, saw Sunyata's distress as she was being pulled farther and farther from shore. The two men, one a police inspector, the other a corrections officer, who were casting their lines from the beach, knew that they had to do something quickly to try to save my daughter as she was being pulled out to sea.

Jacques Snyman cast the line from his fishing rod out past Sunyata and she was able to grab onto it, although, as she tugged, it began to cut into her hand and wrist. Luckily she could wrap part of her skirt around her hand and was able to continue to hold onto the line. Snyman was able to reel her in and both men assisted her ashore where she soon recovered from her ordeal as the paramedics ran down to assist her.

The fishermen reported that the fishing line used was designed only to reel in a fish up to 12 kilograms (24.6 pounds). Sunyata weighs 59 kilograms (130 pounds), over five times the capacity of the line's strength, so there was considerable skill and much luck that allowed Snyman to bring Sunyata ashore.

Ironically, earlier in the month, Sunyata had lectured the two men that it was cruel and unethical to be fishing for sharks in these waters.

Both men were lauded as heroes as the headlines in South African newspapers read: *Catch of the Day*. Needless to say, Sunyata's father back in Canada was most thankful that the two Jacques happened to be out fishing that day and so he dedicated this novel, *Random*, to them.